BACHELOR DOCTOR

When Dr Sara Linford accepts a job in Gavin Morland's practice, she assures him there will be no personal complications. From the start Gavin makes it clear that he is a confirmed bachelor and she herself is dedicated to her career and has no desire for marriage. But Dr Gavin Morland, besides being a confirmed bachelor, is devastatingly attractive—a fact she finds impossible to ignore.

BACHELOR DOCTOR

When Dr Sara Linford accepts a job in Gavin Morland's practice, she assures him there will be no personal complications. From the start Gavin makes it clear that he is a confirmed bachelor and she herself is dedicated to her career and has no desire for marriage. But Dr Gavin Morland, besides being a confirmed bachelor, is devastatingly attractive—a fact she finds impossible to ignore.

BACHELOR DOCTOR

Bachelor Doctor

by
Sonia Deane

Magna Large Print Books
Long Preston, North Yorkshire,
England.

British Library Cataloguing in Publication Data.

Deane, Sonia
   Bachelor doctor.

   A catalogue record for this book is
   available from the British Library

   ISBN 0-7505-1002-1

First published in Great Britain by Mills & Boon Ltd., 1982

Copyright © 1982 by Sonia Deane

The right of Sonia Deane to be identified as the author of this work has been asserted in accordance with the Copyright, Designs and Patents Act, 1988

Published in Large Print September, 1996 by arrangement with Rupert Crew Limited.

Magna Large Print is an imprint of
Library Magna Books Ltd.
Printed and bound in Great Britain by
T.J. Press (Padstow) Ltd., Cornwall, PL28 8RW.

All the characters in this book have no existence outside the imagination of the Author, and have no relation whatsoever to anyone bearing the same name or names. They are not even distantly inspired by any individual known or unknown to the Author, and all the incidents are pure invention.

CHAPTER ONE

Within seconds of seeing the middle-aged man clutch at his chest and slump to the ground, Sara had stopped her car and rushed to his aid, aware that she was dealing with a case of cardiac arrest. She knelt on her left knee at his side, making sure his tongue was brought forward and the airway cleared, before putting her right hand on the right side of the sternum (left hand crossways on top of the right hand) and pumping to the limit of her strength with precision and regularity.

A car braked nearby, and footsteps hurried towards her, a deep reassuring voice saying, 'I'm a doctor.'

'So am I,' she exclaimed without looking up.

'Let me take over while you give mouth to mouth resuscitation.' Strong hands slid into place on the man's chest as Sara obeyed without protest. After what seemed an eternity, and after a final heavy thump, came the relieved cry, 'The pulse is going...must get an ambulance. I'm on an emergency, but I can telephone from that house down the road. I know the people there.'

For a split second, Sara looked up at the figure rising swiftly to his feet as he talked. He was tall, commanding, and, even amid the tension and drama, almost menacingly handsome. He called out as he hurried away, 'You stand by. The depot's not far; he must have oxygen.'

Sara, still on her knees keeping vigil, glanced around at the country lane which was on the fringe of Ledbury in Herefordshire. At that moment it seemed the most desolate lonely place on earth.

An ambulance, siren wailing, arrived with miraculous speed, the patient was skilfully transferred to it, and oxygen administered immediately. Sara accompanied him. She could, she reflected, supply the details and possibly speak to the relatives. A wave of disappointment momentarily took the place of anxiety. She didn't even know the name of the doctor who had helped her. It also registered that she had left her car parked by the roadside and would eventually have to collect it!

'Eventually' turned out to be about forty

minutes later. The patient, named Robert Miles, was known at the South Cotswold Hospital and taken quickly into Intensive Care. The particulars Sara was able to give were duly noted, and a porter detailed to get her a taxi. When finally she returned to her car and sank into the driving seat, a feeling of unreality stole over her. The peaceful silence of the summer afternoon seemed incongruous. A faint breeze stirred hedgerow and wildflowers, and the faint smell of honeysuckle wafted from an invisible farm cottage. *'I'm a doctor.'* She heard the echo of those words uttered in a resonant voice she would never forget. It didn't matter how grim the circumstances, the unknown doctor's presence lingered as though by some mysterious and magnetic force. And now, she thought almost rebelliously, she had to go for an interview with a view to joining a practice in Ledbury! The prospect didn't appeal, even though she wanted the job. But it struck her that she might well be able to discover the identity of the man whose brief acquaintance had made such an impression. Dr Gavin Morland—her prospective employer—was bound to know his medical colleagues in the area.

The Morland house, Tudor Court, stood at the corner of a quiet clearing near the High Street, peeping from a magnificent screen of beech trees through which the afternoon sun filtered like golden rain. Sara parked her car in the short drive, squared her shoulders and fortified herself with the knowledge that she had no need to accept any position unless it appealed to her. She was neither penniless nor homeless!

The door bell of the half-timbered black-and-white dwelling was answered by a white-jacketed manservant who showed her into a spacious drawing-room that had a lived-in, comfortable atmosphere, enhanced by the mellowness and permanence of antiques.

'Dr Morland will be back shortly.'

Sara smiled, and moved to the window which overlooked a large walled-in garden, massed with bloom. A sun-dial and lily pond could be glimpsed in the near distance, and a cushioned hammock offered sanctuary beneath a sturdy elm. Some minutes later the door opened and a voice which set her nerves tingling said, 'So we meet again. I recognised your car!'

Sara stared at the man aghast, 'But you're not—'

'I'm Dr Morland—Gavin Morland—yes.'

Standing there he seemed to possess a strength and fascination far in excess of that which she remembered. And while she told herself it was ridiculous to be attracted to a man she had seen for such a brief while earlier that afternoon, nevertheless excitement surged as she exclaimed, 'I suppose it was inevitable that we should meet again—two doctors in a small market town.' She laughed, 'I wondered if "Dr Morland" might satisfy my curiosity about your identity!' She added swiftly, 'I'm Sara Linford.'

'So your application divulged!' He smiled.

'Of course, how silly of me!'

'And our patient?'

Sara explained, finishing with, 'That last thump of yours was just what the doctor ordered! Actually, it was my first roadside emergency...I'm surprised you recognised my car.'

'One takes note of things without seeming to observe them.' He paused. 'And it *is* a rather startling red!' There was no criticism implied in the remark.

'It was the only colour available in the make I wanted.' She wondered just what kind of man she was dealing with. The impact of his personality overwhelmed her. Voice, manner, appearance, all conspired to build up a picture of an unusual and impressive character. The first shock of seeing him again vanished as she studied him more closely aware that, while he suggested friendliness, there was a guarded expression in his grey eyes and a faint aloofness in his attitude which was at variance with his actual words. Not, she decided, someone easy to assess.

'Now,' he began, when they were comfortably seated in their respective chairs. 'To begin with, this isn't a conveyor-belt practice with an overloaded list. I've no intention of running a group practice. My father was here before me and, rightly or wrongly, the patients want to see me, and I like it that way. Even so, there are limits, and I need a woman to deal with the gynaecological side... Oh, not exclusively, but in the main. You have your midwifery, which is vital.' He paused. 'How do you feel about working with just one other person?'

'Relieved at the prospect. I've had enough of hospital life and, as I told you in my letter, I've done locum work. There were five partners in the last practice. It was hectic and it was not possible to give the patients the attention they needed.'

Sara knew that he was weighing up every word she uttered, but it was impossible to gauge his reactions. Was he married? A tremor went over her. She felt instinctively that he would not appreciate being questioned on the subject.

'I notice that you live in London,' he said. 'Why do you want to come to Ledbury?'

His magnetic penetrating eyes met hers almost challengingly; his voice was firm almost to the point of cross-examination.

'Firstly, because I prefer the country and, secondly, because my aunt has moved here and I am going to live with her. My parents are dead.' She hastened, 'I shall have my own rooms and be quite free. I've shared with her before, so it is not an experiment.'

Gavin Morland had lowered his gaze and raised it disconcertingly to meet hers, 'I don't want to take on anyone who is thinking in terms of marriage,' he said doggedly. 'I'm a bachelor.' He spoke as though she had a right to know. 'We've enough problems with the patients, without creating our own.' He didn't remove his eyes from her face. 'Let there be no misunderstanding on that issue. If you are—'

She cut in, a little spark of annoyance flaming within her, 'I'm not involved in any emotional entanglement, or likely to be, Dr Morland, if that is what you mean. I want to work, gain experience.' She added, 'I'm certainly not in search of a husband, I assure you.'

He liked the flicker of anger in her dark lustrous eyes; the way her head lifted slightly in a gesture of defiance. The sun glinted on her long, silky dark hair, which had auburn tints as though golden cobwebs lay upon it. He decided that she had strength of character, poise and frankness.

'Then I see no reason why we should not make a good team—if you are in agreement.'

Excitement flooded over her, but she said smoothly, 'Yes; I'm in agreement.' She added swiftly, 'But it would be rather difficult for me to start until next month.'

'No problem there,' he reassured her. 'Shall we say July 1st?'

'That would be ideal.'

'And gives you a little over two weeks.'

'I've to move from the London flat which I've shared with two friends,' Sara explained.

He nodded his understanding. Then, 'I have the one secretary-cum-factotum—Mrs Reece, an elderly lady—my manservant, Bates, whom you've already met; and a daily helper. It all works extremely well.' His smile was slow and reflective, 'I might add that Mrs Reece is faintly suspicious of my taking an assistant, she's been here too long to accept change without fear.'

'Then it will be up to me to allay those fears.'

'I'm confident you will do that,' he said. 'How about a drink? No surgery tonight, so I'm free.' He walked to the drinks tray and looked back at her.

'A dry sherry, please.' She watched his broad-shouldered lithe figure; her thoughts and emotions chaotic as she realised that this was the man for whom she was going to work. *'I'm a bachelor,'* The words spun in her head; but the fact lent a certain intimacy to the situation, and while she accepted that it was always dangerous to be emotionally involved with any working associate, nevertheless, she argued, without danger, relationships could be like eggs without salt. Dr Gavin Morland was not a man one could contemplate dispassionately; he dominated the scene like an actor bringing a play to life, leaving it bereft when he was not on the stage. His gaze made her aware of her heart and the quickening of her pulse, and as she took the drink it was with difficulty that she managed to keep her hand steady. How many other people had he interviewed? Why had he chosen her? His provocative aloofness forbade her asking for reasons. It was enough that he wanted her to join him.

'It's excellent,' he said smoothly, 'that you are settling here. The problem of where to live isn't simple in these days.'

'My aunt's house is on the Eastnor Road—only about a mile away.'

'So you know the area well?'

'Yes.'

He was watching her with thoughtful

contemplation, and said somewhat disarmingly, 'Thank heaven, the future is settled. I don't like wasting time with non-productive interviews. Some of the applicants might have been about to join a night club!'

'The inference being that you do not believe in mixing business with pleasure?' The tone of her voice made the statement a question.

She saw his jaw harden, and a rather fierce expression darken his eyes.

'Precisely. That is a recipe for disaster.' It was a bold crisp statement uttered with finality. 'An atmosphere of friendly co-operation is another matter.'

'Such as enjoying a glass of sherry,' she suggested significantly.

He inclined his head in agreement. 'Exactly.'

Sara finished the drink and said in businesslike tone, 'I must be going.'

He got immediately to his feet as she moved from her chair.

'Until July 1st,' he said, walking with her to the front door and seeing her to her car. There she turned, looked at him, and extended her hand.

'Goodbye, Dr Morland.'

His touch filled her with a sudden electrifying emotion. For a second he looked at her, the gaze holding, his expression registering a degree of surprise. Then their hands loosened their tight, almost intimate grip, falling apart as thought the contact burned them.

'It has been a strange coincidence,' he said, half-superstitiously, looking at her car with lingering amazement. 'I should certainly know it anywhere.'

'Then there's no hope of my escaping surveillance,' she retorted.

'None, Dr Linford.' A faint smile cut through the formality.

'Incidentally, my aunt's address, should you have any reason to contact me, is just Thatched Cottage, Eastnor. Her name is Kate Wilton, she's a widow. It would be stretching coincidence too far if you should know of her.'

Gavin Morland shook his head. 'We'll be satisfied with the one coincidence.' His grey eyes seemed suddenly cold and remote. 'Goodbye.' He shut the car door and stood back as Sara drove off, striding into the house without a backward glance.

Sara didn't see Gavin Morland again until the end of June, when she had finally settled in at Thatched Cottage in what was virtually a suite of her own, which had been built on by the previous owners for their guests. He arrived unexpectedly, walking across the lawns towards her as she lay sunbathing. And while he appeared not to be aware of her slim, yet voluptuous, body, sensuously tanned, Sara nevertheless had the feeling that his gaze had taken in every curve of her figure which was clad in three triangles of blue material.

'I saw you through the trees from the drive,' he explained.

Sara sat up and slipped a flimsy poncho over her head. Had he come to make a change of plan? Her heart sank at the possibility. She indicated a nearby deck-chair and he sat down, adding, 'I was passing...' He left the sentence in mid-air, not wanting to explain that he had acted on impulse.

Sara drew her knees up to her chin and clasped her arms around her legs, surveying him while trying to control the emotion surging through her.

'You haven't changed your mind about wanting me to join you next week?' The words slipped out, conveying anxiety.

'Good heavens, no. If anything, I

suppose I wanted to make sure that you were installed here.' It was an admission that surprised him. He couldn't have said why, on the spur of the moment, he had turned into the drive of Thatched Cottage.

He looked down at her and their eyes met in a significant gaze, acute awareness of each other flashing between them.

Kate Wilton appeared from an adjoining lavender garden. Sara made the necessary introduction. Kate was welcoming; fifty-five, grey-haired thoroughly modern, while more than intrigued by her niece's employer who looked strikingly handsome as he got to his feet.

'It's long past drinks time,' she announced. 'You'll join us, Dr Morland?'

'Thank you.'

'Shall we go inside?' Kate gave a chuckle as she looked at Sara. 'My niece behaves as though she was born in the tropics!'

'All the same, I've had enough sun for this morning,' Sara retorted. 'I'll change and join you.' With that she ran across the velvet lawns, hurried up to her bedroom and emerged in the drawing-room looking cool and alluring in a crisp cream dress that emphasised her nut-brown skin.

'We're having white wine,' Kate announced. 'Something chilled is refreshing on a day like this.'

Sara agreed; but she was hardly conscious of what she wished to drink, the phrase, '*I was passing*', seemed to open up infinite possibilities and contradict the rigid discipline of not mixing business with pleasure. The last thing she had envisaged was Gavin Morland at the cottage! He seemed to give a new dimension to the room, which was oak-beamed, latticed, and with a massive chimney corner. He sat deep in his chair, yet, she thought, watchful. Every time his eyes met hers it was as though her heart paused and adjusted to the fierce emotion that suffused her body.

'This is ideal,' he exclaimed appreciatively, glancing at his wine. 'I've just come from a mid-der—a boy—and already wetted the baby's head!'

Kate said enthusiastically, 'I think doctors are marvellous people. I never thought my niece would become one, but I'm proud of the fact, and don't mind admitting it!'

'And I'm *grateful* for the fact,' Gavin Morland said immediately. 'Otherwise I might still be looking for someone to share the work-load!'

Sara heard the words with unashamed pleasure, conscious of his every movement, aware of his casual clothes which nevertheless managed to look well-groomed, his commanding presence lending authority even to a commonplace utterance.

'This is a delightful cottage,' he said a little later.

'Thatched, without the thatch!' Kate laughed. 'It's very old, and there isn't an even floor in the place; but I love it... Could you stay to lunch, Dr Morland?'

Sara tensed, her gaze flying to his.

There was an imperceptible pause before he replied smoothly, 'Thank you all the same, but I'm having a working lunch with a colleague.'

Was that an excuse? Sara asked herself. It was suddenly impossible to tell by his expression whether there was an element of regret in the statement. And then he looked straight into her eyes, as though aware of her thoughts, while having no intention of betraying his own.

Kate asked unexpectedly and with interest, 'Have you by any chance a relative living at Hay-on-Wye, Dr Morland?'

The sudden silence was deep and uneasy. A blind came down over Gavin Morland's face; his eyes hardened, his manner changing to a cold remoteness. When he spoke, his words came with clipped precision.

'My brother, Stewart, lives there. His field is anaesthetics.' It was as though he added, 'And I've no intention of discussing him.'

'Just,' Kate hastened, 'that a friend of mine happens to know him...I'm finding it very interesting to explore Herefordshire and get to know something of Wales,' she hurried on, anxious to convey that she respected his reluctance to discuss his brother.

'I envy you your enthusiasm,' he said sombrely. 'And now I'm afraid I must be going.'

Sara looked at him and felt that he had suddenly become a stranger. She walked with him to his car, hating the bleak sensation that his solemnity aroused. Yet solemnity, she argued, was not quite the right word. It was as if he had moved to another place.

'I'm glad you have such a pleasant and happy background,' he said unexpectedly as he opened his car door.

'I appreciate it,' she said with feeling,

her gaze going to his, but while he looked at her, his expression told her nothing.

'Until Wednesday,' he said politely. 'It would be a good idea if you could look in before then—to get acquainted with the place. I didn't show you where you would be working.' He glanced down at her speculatively. 'Would tomorrow evening suit you? After surgery—say about seven.'

'Very well.'

He nodded without smiling. And as he drove away she told herself that he wouldn't be an easy man to work with, while knowing that his unpredictability would represent a challenge she was more than ready to accept.

Over lunch Kate said with a wry smile, 'I put my foot in it over the brother.'

'Probably because he doesn't want any gossip.'

Her aunt's reply was nothing Sara might have expected as she said, 'You've certainly hit the nail on the head there...'

'What makes you say that?' Sara spoke in a breath that held a note of apprehension.

'Nothing really; just that Dr Morland is supposed to be the confirmed bachelor-cum-woman-hater because of a disastrous love affair that happened some years ago.'

'Doesn't strike me as a woman hater.'

Kate asked herself if the remark was wishful thinking. 'Anyway,' she said with a smile, 'he's an extraordinarily attractive man. Unusual and intriguing. Working for him will certainly not be dull!'

'Who told you about his love affair? Someone who's probably never met him!'

'On the contrary, it was Ruth Dexter—'

'Your friend at Hay?'

'Yes. Stewart Morland told her himself, and that could hardly be likened to gossip!'

'Why didn't you mention it before?' Sara spoke half-reproachfully.

'Because it was only discussed when I was at Hay yesterday,' Kay retorted with a laugh. 'I should have told you over our drinks this morning. It's hardly world-shattering news, anyway.' She eyed Sara speculatively, 'Unless you are inordinately interested in Dr Morland's love life!'

Sara scoffed, 'Oh Kate, don't be silly... What does Ruth think of my joining the Ledbury practice?'

'She's delighted—simply because it means your living here with me.'

'Is she likely to have told Stewart Morland that I'm joining his brother?'

Kate didn't hesitate. 'I very much doubt

it. Ruth rarely discusses the affairs of her friends.'

'Not that it matters,' Sara hastened. 'In any case news travels very fast in medical circles.'

'And in any other circles,' chortled Kate. 'I thought you said that Dr Morland had rigid views about not mixing business with pleasure...that being so, what brought him here today?'

Sara flushed.

'He said he was passing. I was amazed to see him.'

Kate puckered her brows. 'I'm glad to have met him. Difficult man to judge, beyond the fact that he's a handsome, aggressively masculine brute!'

Sara changed the subject.

The following evening she arrived at Tudor Court punctually at seven. Her reception was businesslike. There was a comfortable homeliness about the practice rooms, and even the surgery waiting room escaped the bare clinical dreariness that often struck chill at the heart of the patients.

'Mrs Reece always sees that there are flowers in here, and that the magazines are not dog-eared and outdated.'

'Atmosphere counts so much,' Sara exclaimed. 'There is an air of friendliness about it all.'

'Does that surprise you?' The question was a trifle sharp.

'*Pleases* would be a better word.'

'And an evasion,' he suggested, and while he did not smile, he conveyed acquiescence.

Sara found her room far better than she had hoped. It was light, airy, white-walled and well appointed; a room she could make her own with a few little touches at which she was adept.

As though reading her thoughts, he said, 'You can re-arrange things as you wish, and ask for anything you feel is missing, or lacking. People work better in congenial surroundings.'

'Thank you,' she said warmly.

He looked at her with directness almost for the first time since her arrival.

'I appreciate your sensitivity. It is a quality that cannot be acquired.'

The understanding heartened her. This man was full of surprises. Would he ask her to stay for a drink, she wondered, when, finally, he showed her his consulting room which was oak-panelled and faced the rose garden. *'A confirmed bachelor-cum-woman-hater because of a disastrous love affair.'* The words echoed significantly and she was consumed with curiosity. There were only two photographs on the chimney piece; photographs that would appear to be of his parents.

'I have made a list of the patients I want you to look after,' he said as he shut his consulting-room door. 'Mrs Reece will give you their case notes. Every new patient must be thoroughly examined. A pain-killer, or tranquillizer, will not do. Above all, explain what is wrong and don't hide behind mumbo-jumbo. Half the uncertainty and mental distress is caused by the patient not knowing what is wrong. People don't like to be kept in the dark; ignorance breeds distrust and magnifies fears. And that doesn't mean not using discretion when something grave is at stake.' He looked at her levelly. 'Is that clear?'

'Perfectly,' She nodded her agreement.

'Good.' He studied her with professional assessment suggesting that he was well satisfied with her reactions. 'Adjustments can be made as you go along.'

He didn't refer to his visit to Thatched

Cottage the previous day; it might not have taken place. They walked side by side from the practice quarters to the square hall where a spiral staircase swept up impressively to the first floor, but all Sara was conscious of was his presence beside her; and his overpowering personality, and physical attraction.

'Thank you for coming,' he said.

He didn't make the words seem like a dismissal, but rather as a polite means of bringing the meeting to an end. She looked up at him and his gaze travelled over her face in sudden awareness, almost as though seeing her for the first time. For a second he hesitated and then said swiftly, 'Goodbye, Dr Linford.' With that he opened the front door. The telephone rang at that moment and murmuring an apology, he hurried to answer it, as Sara left. She stood beside her car for a brief while, taking in the beauty of the scene. The warmth, the fragrance, the golden glow of evening. A feeling of disappointment lurked to mingle with a yearning new and dangerous, as she looked back at the house which whispered of yesterday, yet promised her tomorrow. She would be working there, building her future within its ancient solid walls. *Was* its owner a woman-hater? The possibility was a tantalizing challenge, and colour rose to her cheeks because her thoughts were unruly, her desires sensuous and unfamiliar.

Sara had been in the practice for three months before any note of familiarity was struck. The work had gone smoothly and while she was not praised unduly, neither was she criticised. She had established a rapport and harmony with her patients, won over Mrs Reece, and generally proved herself invaluable.

On this evening in early October, Gavin Morland said, 'I think we deserve a break. It's been a long day. Let's go into the drawing-room and forget work for a change.'

Once there, Sara watched him pour out their respective drinks, her thoughts rushing back to the first time she had met him, her gaze seeking his as she took her sherry and said, 'At least we haven't had any more roadside patients!'

'I was just remembering that day,' he admitted, 'and thinking it is about time that we resorted to Christian names! The "doctor" has become rather stilted!'

It was the last thing Sara had expected, or even contemplated. During the past months she had been deliberately formal, her approach to him strictly professional, and she had learned no more about him during that time than on the day she first joined him. There was a degree of humour between them for which she was thankful, but she had been determined not to place herself in the position where he might accuse her of introducing an emotional familiarity calculated to romanticise their association. A rebuff would have been unendurable.

Her silence prompted his, 'Do you agree?'

'By all means. I've merely respected your desire for a strictly professional attitude.' Her voice was even, her expression bland, but her heart was racing, excitement creeping upon her.

'An attitude I've appreciated...you probably think me unnecessarily formal.' His gaze held hers inescapably.

'I think you have a right to make the rules,' she replied.

'And should you disagree with them?' he prompted, his voice low and conciliatory.

'I can say so, or—' She paused.

'Seek another practice,' he finished swiftly.

'That is certainly a possibility...but not very likely at the moment.'

He arched his brows and continued to study her, the atmosphere electric.

'I'm glad of that,' he said. 'I shouldn't like the pattern to change, Sara.'

Her name sounded like a caress which echoed between them, endangering their reserve.

'Nothing, stands still,' she said quietly.

He said almost roughly, 'That is one of the tragedies of life.'

'Meaning that you want eternal fidelity?' The words hung dangerously between them, smashing the protective wall of restraint that had built up around them.

'Is the idea of it so foreign to you?' His voice was harsh, almost accusing.

'That depends on the circumstances.' It was obvious that, for him, the conversation was not merely an exchange of views, but a fundamental betrayal of his own deep-rooted disillusionment and anger.

'Convenient compromise,' he retorted with disgust.

'On the contrary, Gavin—a recognition of reality.'

They looked at each other, eyes flashing; emotion surging into passionate revelation. She ached to be in his arms; to feel the touch of his lips and the hardness of his body. Attraction was searing and agonising.

And suddenly, like a man defeated, he said with a sigh, 'You're right, of course. In the final analysis we have to live with reality.' Even as he spoke his expression changed and he returned to his private world, shutting the door behind him.

Sara was trembling, engulfed by feelings deep, tortuous and inexplicable. She might have been under a spell and in the power of this man who could set her heart racing with a look, and her body quivering at the thought of his caress.

Silently he took their glasses and refilled them, impressive even in his apparent calm.

The bell rang, alerting them to a possible emergency, followed by the sound of Bates greeting someone obviously familiar to him.

'My brother,' Gavin said, tight-lipped.

Sara started in surprise.

'We do meet—very occasionally... Hello, Stewart,' as Stewart came into the room.

Gavin's voice was neither openly hostile, nor welcoming.

Stewart moved forward with an easy grace. He was self-confident and self-possessed.

'And this, I presume, is Dr Linford?' Stewart smiled at Sara and there was obvious admiration in his eyes. 'I heard that you had acquired a beautiful assistant,' he added, addressing Gavin. 'Gossip, for once, was correct.'

No two men, Sara thought, could have been so dissimilar.

'I've been here for three months,' she exclaimed, slightly embarrassed by the obvious flattery.

'Then I've been very remiss in not calling before...' He paused. 'Tudor Court will act as a magnet in future. Gavin and I don't see half as much of each other as we ought to do...particularly as we are the only surviving members of the family... A whisky, Gavin, please.' He looked into Sara's eyes. 'I'm sure you're finding my brother a very dedicated doctor. Long hours; good to old ladies; but very secretive. Strong silent man stuff!' He took the whisky glass and settled lazily in an arm-chair. His fair hair caught the glint of the evening sun; he suggested the pleasure-seeker to whom life was a game.

'I must be going,' said Sara with resolution. She got to her feet as she spoke; both men rising as she did so.

Stewart protested, 'Surely I am not driving you away?' It was an aggrieved sound. 'Why don't we three go out to dinner? I know of—'

'Thank you,' Sara interrupted, 'but my aunt is expecting me; we have guests... Goodbye, Dr Stewart,' she said deliberately; 'we can't have two Dr *Morlands* in the house.'

'But you'll be seeing more of *this* Dr Morland, I warn you,' Stewart said significantly, holding Sara's hand a fraction longer than was necessary.

Gavin saw Sara to the door.

'I'm sorry about that,' he murmured, hastening, 'It must be five or six months since my brother has been here.' There was a dark impatience in Gavin's eyes, and faint hostility in his voice.

'He is very charming,' Sara said spontaneously, finding that the words Stewart had uttered about Gavin, *'but very secretive'*, made her resentful to the point where she was prepared for dissension or argument.

Gavin's jaw clenched; he stood there aggressive and dangerous in his calm.

'Goodnight, Sara.' He gave her name importance, and for a second was so near that their hands touched and convulsively clasped as passion swept between them in a shuddering spasm.

'Goodnight, Gavin,' she whispered, and hurried from the door to her car, starting it as confusion, excitement and desire flooded over her. No man had ever roused her as this man was capable of doing, she thought, almost rebelliously; or left her so completely ignorant of his feelings, thoughts, intentions.

It was the following week and at the end of a particularly hard afternoon, that Mrs Reece—brisk, efficient, spectacles hanging on a chain around her neck, wispy hair fluffing out from her face—said to Sara, 'Oh, Dr Linford, there's a patient waiting to see Dr Morland. A Mrs Howard...she has a little girl with her and was most insistent...I told her that the doctor was attending an emergency operation, but she was quite adamant... If you would have a word with her...'

Sara went into the waiting room. 'I'm Dr Linford,' she began brightly, 'can I help you?' She studied the woman sitting determinedly, the child of about four on her lap. She had an unusual face, devoid of make-up, with large, dark brown eyes that looked more accustomed to sorrow than happiness.

'It is Dr Morland I want to see. I've come from Builth Wells.' The voice was gentle, but persistent. 'I'm a friend of his,' she added firmly. 'My car broke down, or I should have been here at a more reasonable hour.'

'You must come through to the drawing-room and wait there.' Sara made the decision instinctively, impressed by Marion Howard's attitude which held a certain forbearance.

'I'm hungry,' complained the child, wriggling down from its mother's lap and standing looking up expectantly at Sara, a rather woebegone expression on its round, cherub-like face with its frame of dark, page-boy-cut hair.

'Becky!' the mother exclaimed with quiet admonishment.

'And I'm sure you would both like some tea,' Sara suggested, and led the way to the drawing-room, immediately ordering tea and cakes from a somewhat startled Bates.

Becky settled herself in a small chair and smoothed her blue smocked dress with a certain fastidious precision. Her gaze didn't leave Sara's face.

'Do you live here?' she asked.

'No,' Sara said with a smile.

'Where do you live?'

'At my aunt's house in Ledbury.'

'We live in Wales.' It was announced with a degree of importance. 'My daddy's dead,' she added solemnly. Her lower lip puckered, tears filled her eyes. 'I don't like him being dead.'

'I'm sorry.' Sara's gaze went to Marion Howard's face and a strange sensation of foreboding struck.

'Six weeks ago.' It was a quiet dejected utterance.

A car drew up in the drive.

'That is probably Dr Morland,' Sara hastened.

Gavin hurried into the house and to the drawing-room. At the sight of Marion Howard and Becky he stopped, seemingly frozen to the spot. Then he gasped, 'Marion! *You!*' His expression was shocked and disbelieving; the atmosphere electric.

Sarah went unnoticed from the room.

CHAPTER TWO

Sara waited, tense and impatient, for Gavin to appear after Marion Howard's car eventually drove away. It was almost time for surgery when he strode through into the waiting room, glanced at Sara as she hovered in readiness, and said flatly, 'We can open up.'

She looked at him half-questioningly. Surely he would mention Marion Howard?

But he didn't; neither did he make any further comment before disappearing into his consulting room.

She flushed as she pulled back the bolt from the surgery door. Why, after all, should he take her into his confidence other than in a professional capacity? Nevertheless she could not forget the expression on his face as he cried, 'Marion—*you!*' Where did a young widow and small child fit into his bachelor life unless, of course, the late Mr Howard had been a friend of his? But while that likely explanation negatived the possibility of drama, it in no way satisfied Sara's curiosity.

Patients were few that evening. A sore throat; 'me veins, doctor'; a self-diagnosed appendicitis, which was no more than an upset stomach; a worn-out mother, trying to cope with an alcoholic husband and a spina-bifida child; an anorexia nervosa, starving to keep slim and, finally, a distracted mother, fearful that her defiant unruly sixteen-year-old daughter was pregnant—a suspicion confirmed, amid protestations, abuse and hysterics.

Gavin had infinite patience, and a flair for dealing with adolescents and, as Sara assisted him, she was struck by the gentleness and amazing understanding he betrayed even to patients least deserving of sympathy.

'I'm glad,' he said unexpectedly (when the surgery door was once again bolted and he and Sara were alone in his consulting room) 'to be spared any more cases this evening.' An expression of weariness shadowed his features as he cupped his chin in his hands and rested his elbows on his desk. 'It's been quite a day, one way and another.' His gaze lifted to look directly at Sara, as he added, his voice low, almost appealing, 'Come out to dinner with me; I don't feel like eating alone.'

Surprise flashed into Sara's eyes. This was not the man who had insisted on a purely businesslike relationship.

'I'd like to,' she replied, her pulse quickening.

He brightened. 'We could go to The Cottage in the Wood at Malvern Wells.' His enthusiasm waned and he stopped abruptly, a faintly self-conscious air accompanying his apologetic, 'I'm sorry, I'd overlooked a telephone call...I must be here...would you mind staying in? Bates is an excellent chef, I assure you. We'll make an occasion of going to The Cottage sometime. It's an hotel to savour.' He appeared to hang anxiously on her reply.

Sara assured him that she would be happy to stay in. But her real interest centred around the telephone call which, obviously, was not connected with a patient, or he would automatically have mentioned the fact. There was a degree of uncertainty, even mystery, in the atmosphere, and his manner seemed wholly out of character as they went through into the drawing-room.

'Whisky for me,' he said. 'Would you

like a change from your sherry?'

'No, thank you.' She took the sherry and settled in her chair, watching him carefully as he rang for Bates and acquainted him with the fact that Sara would be remaining. While he spoke perfectly normally, there was a certain distraction about him, as though his thoughts were far removed from his words.

A sudden uncomfortable silence fell as Bates left them.

'There is one great drawback about living alone,' he said unexpectedly.

'Such as?'

'Eating alone,' he admitted.

'One can never have the best of both worlds,' Sara reminded him succinctly.

A wry attractive smile touched his lips.

'I wonder how sincere we both are when it comes to prizing our freedom.' The remark was without aggression, rather was it in the nature of genuine assessment, even self-criticism.

'As sincere as any two people can be when their respective freedom isn't threatened,' she said with a smooth conviction, and then found herself hovering on the edge of apprehension. Had renewing his relationship with Marion Howard stimulated his remark?

'One's freedom is always threatened,' he said, holding her gaze. 'If only by the weakness of human nature.'

'And the power of emotion,' she added.

'Emotion,' he reminded her, 'lies at the root of all human weakness. That is what makes us so defensive when we try to fight it.'

The tension crept stealthily between them, seeming to take all the air from the room. Sara tried to remove her gaze from his, but he seemed to be holding it by magnetic force. 'I should think *you* would always be able to avoid it, nevertheless,' she managed to say in a low voice.

'Is that a challenge?' The words echoed in the silence, increasing her heartbeat and sending a little shiver of desire over her body.

'On the contrary. It is a logical conclusion based on the assessment of months.' And even as she spoke, Sara heard the echo of her aunt's words, 'A confirmed bachelor-cum-woman-hater because of a disastrous love affair.' A thought struck shatteringly: Had Marion Howard been involved in that love affair?

'My suggestion that we have dinner

together has certainly stimulated some interesting ideas,' Gavin commented.

As he spoke he studied her with mesmeric intensity, while emotion built up between them with slow insidious power, until at last he got up abruptly from his chair and walked to the drinks tray as though unable to endure the tension.

Sara sat there, aware only of his presence. He turned and looked back at her, tipping a small amount of whisky into his glass, and then re-filling hers with slow deliberation, like a man playing for time in which to regain his composure; but the memory of that total physical commitment hung between them like the notes of a haunting melody.

'To mix business with pleasure is a receipt for disaster,' he had said to her, she reflected. Was she now throwing herself headlong into that same disaster, his fascination robbing her of willpower or common sense? But there was something magical about the glow of that October evening which enthralled her as she allowed her gaze to lose itself in his and, in doing so, betrayed all the passion and longing that was flowing over her tense body as though his hands had already caressed her.

At that moment Bates interrupted them and they went silently into the candle-lit dining-room. The wine was decanted and the cut-glass shimmered like illuminated cobwebs against the silver and napery.

'How beautiful it all looks,' Sara murmured.

'Bates will have been in his element,' Gavin said. 'He deplores the fact that I have so few people here.'

The curtains had not been drawn and the grounds lay in the serenity and hush of the after-glow, spilling its soft rose light upon the burnished trees like flames rising from the dark rich earth—mysterious and awe-inspiring. Wood-smoke hung in the air, its smell holding the tang of autumn. And even as she watched, darkness seemed suddenly to fall; shadows vanishing, the silence becoming absolute.

When the meal was over they lingered at the table, reluctant to break the spell that lay upon them. Gavin betrayed an entirely different facet of his character during that time, the withdrawn, often curt manner giving way to a gentle sympathetic understanding that enhanced his attraction, and increased her curiosity about his life. Curiosity didn't seem quite the right description and she retreated from it without finding a substitute. All she knew was that her interest, and desire to know him better, deepened, making her doubly vulnerable to his strong physical appeal.

'I'm glad we didn't go out,' she said softly, her gaze seeking his in the flickering candlelight.

'So am I,' he agreed, adding softly, 'there are stars in your eyes, Sara.'

'Candlelight can be very alluring.'

'So can you,' he said with unexpected intensity.

Silence fell. They looked at each other as though exploring a new world, thrilled by its discovery and desirous to the point of pain. Sara had never experienced a physical attraction that completely overwhelmed her, or met a man like Gavin who, while stimulating her senses, nevertheless also aroused a degree of fear. She wanted him to make love to her; she wanted the warmth and hardness of his body against hers; and the fact that they were sitting decorously at the dinner table made no difference. Time and place had ceased to exist.

They returned to the drawing-room, and suddenly, with an upsurge of emotion, he

48

drew her into his arms, his lips touching hers and then parting them in a deep searching kiss that made her cling to him in a frenzy of passion and desire. Their bodies tensed and pressed closer; his arms held her fiercely and possessively, but as she murmured his name, the telephone rang, echoing through the house—shrill and strident.

Gavin released her abruptly, moving to the door and saying with a slightly confused apology, 'I'm sorry...I'll take it in my room.'

The call was on his private line and Sara knew that he must have deliberately refrained from switching it over. The bell could be heard anywhere. A little shiver of disappointment, tinged with apprehension, went over her, but she managed to look composed as Gavin left and Bates brought in the coffee.

When Gavin returned about ten minutes later, Sara looked at him across what seemed to be an empty room. The ecstasy had vanished.

He avoided her eyes and indicated the silver tray. 'You shouldn't have waited...my apologies,' he murmured, and automatically began pouring, handing her the cup and holding out the cream-jug somewhat distractedly.

'Black,' Sara prompted.

'Of course,' he hastened, remembering, but still avoiding her gaze.

'And you don't take sugar,' she reminded him as he was about to help himself to it.

He gave a little chuckle of self-ridicule, turned, and stood with his back to the chimney-piece, drinking as he did so and seeming to be in another world. The silence was so deep that the ticking of the grandfather clock filled the room with sound.

And then suddenly he looked at her, intently and with a degree of hopeful appeal. She felt that he was willing her to regard the intimacy of that earlier scene as representing nothing more than a flirtatious moment devoid of any dramatic or emotional significance.

She took a deep breath and rose to the occasion.

'I think,' she said, her voice even, her expression pleasant, 'that we're going to have trouble with Mrs Lock.' Sara knew that she could not go wrong in introducing a professional note.

50

Gavin relaxed visibly, his shoulders dropping, a look of relief spreading over his features. A delicate interlude had been erased without repercussion. Inwardly he admired Sara's *sang froid*.

'Mrs Lock is always a problem,' he said, adding injudiciously, 'far too emotional—' He stopped, then, 'I think a brandy would be a good idea.'

'So do I,' Sara agreed brightly, but her heart was pounding and she was conscious of his every movement.

He flashed her a discerning and appreciative glance, poured out the brandies and raised his glass, studying her with renewed interest. When he spoke there was reluctance in his words, 'Life is a contrary business; full of unexpected hazards.'

'The cliché that it is also what we make it has a certain validity nevertheless,' she suggested.

He savoured his brandy, reflective, sombre.

'True; thus our follies are perpetuated.'

'Then I must be glad that I haven't any follies to catch up with me,' she countered, and managed to give a little laugh. 'But I've plenty of time to change the pattern!'

He said almost sternly and with obvious feeling, 'Don't attempt to change it. There's no merit, or satisfaction, in folly.' His eyes darkened as he spoke, the fervour of his words echoing through the silence on a warning note.

Sara realised that she would have to learn to master emotion that almost stifled her. It was impossible to forget those moments in his arms. He confounded her as she looked at him. Was it possible that a telephone call could shatter a mood and kill all desire? The man with whom she had just dined was exciting, fascinating, and entirely different from the reserved, somewhat aggressive Dr Morland she had hitherto known. The former had betrayed a gentleness which she had come to associate with his treatment of his patients—their prerogative which she had often envied. Having betrayed warmth and understanding, could he now return to that hard shell, putting the universe between them while, contradictorily, still allowing the breath of desire to touch some seconds with magic? Did he now regard having kissed her as folly?

'That I shall have to learn for myself,' she commented. 'Folly means something different to each one of us.'

Their eyes met, and again she felt the power of the attraction between them, watching him avert his gaze and concentrate on his drink.

The telephone ringing on the house line evoked a groan from him. He answered it and then said with abrupt surprise, 'Stewart!...I agree; you seldom ring here. What can I do for you?' There was no pleasure in Gavin's voice, merely politeness. 'Sara? Why, yes, as it happens.' There was astonishment in the utterance. 'One moment.' He handed Sara the receiver with a somewhat impatient inquiring gesture. 'For you.'

Sara, startled, nervous, and acutely conscious of Gavin's disapproval, greeted Stewart with bewilderment.

Stewart said, 'I've been ringing Thatched Cottage, but there was no reply, so I took a chance that you might be with my dear brother—probably being worked to death... How about dinner on Saturday?' He made the suggestion sound as thought they were already established friends and that he was merely sustaining a habit.

'Dinner!' The exclamation held confusion.

'I'll pick you up at seven.' It was a *fait accompli*.

'But I—'

'Seven,' he said with smooth determination. 'I told you that you would be seeing more of me.'

Sara felt tongue-tied and awkward, while acutely aware of Gavin's frosty gaze, which roused her to defiance. After all, Stewart's persistence was both effective and flattering.

'Very well; seven at Thatched Cottage.'

'Splendid...*au revoir,* Sara.'

She replaced the receiver, somewhat distracted.

Gavin poured himself out another cup of coffee as he said, 'I wasn't aware you were seeing my brother.'

'I'm not "seeing him". The call was totally unexpected.' She added, 'Do I detect disapproval in your voice?'

'It is not for me to approve or disapprove. Just so long as we don't have the complication of family involvements.'

Sara flashed back, 'Such as not mixing business with pleasure.' Her gaze was direct and unnerving.

'The wisdom implicit in a belief is not diluted because of one's inability to adhere to it on occasion,' he suggested significantly and pedantically.

In the silence that fell between them there was the memory of their kiss and, for a second, passion flowed back.

'I hardly think that my having dinner with your brother will cause a major professional disaster,' she quipped. 'It's been very much all work and no play recently.' She hastened, 'Oh, please don't get me wrong; working hard is a pleasure, but I don't want to become a cabbage in my private life. Stewart makes even saying "Hello", sound like the beginning of a party.'

'Are you usually so precise in your judgements?'

Sara looked at him with quiet assessment.

'No: but your brother struck me as a most entertaining man.'

'Oh! You are right there. Stewart can charm the birds off the trees.'

'A barbed compliment.'

'Not intentionally.'

Sara still held his gaze.

'Your attitude invariably conflicts with your words.'

He smiled unexpectedly.

'No argument.' His voice was slow. 'Attitudes are a spontaneous reaction to circumstances—not always to be trusted.'

Sara felt a slight sickness in the pit of her stomach. It was obvious that he was making an excuse for his own behaviour.

'Perhaps your brother has a more stable view, despite his spontaneity.'

There was a sudden deep silence.

'That you must discover for yourself, Sara.' And while Gavin spoke calmly, there was a note of warning in his voice.

'One can know some people better after five minutes, than others after five years.' She forced a little defiant smile, 'Anyway, you look after your social life, and I'll look after mine!' She added meaningfully, 'The fact that you and your brother are not compatible has nothing to do with me, after all.'

But, again, the memory of that earlier scene lay between them and the silence was filled with emotion.

'And now I must go to see Mrs Grace,' Sara exclaimed with sudden professional concern, conveying that the evening, and the interlude, were over.

Gavin's sigh was deep and solicitous.

'If only we could conquer cancer.'

'The husband won't accept it,' Sara said quietly.

'And yet knows he is deceiving himself;

they've always lived in a fantasy world.'

'Are they less happy on that account?' There was a note of belligerence in Sara's voice.

'"Happy" is a very abused word; who can truthfully say that he, or she, truly comprehends its meaning?'

For once Sara had no desire to challenge him. In the space of an hour or two she had experienced ecstasy, fear, suspense—all concomitants of what was termed 'happiness'. She got up from her chair and Gavin saw her out a few minutes later. There was hesitation between them, as though each expected the other to make some dramatic gesture, but as they reached her car he opened the door, saw her into the driving seat, and said, 'Go carefully.'

'I will.' Her voice was quiet and held the essence of a former magic. Suddenly he leaned forward and put his hand on her, arm. 'Goodnight,' he whispered softly, and stood there as she drove away. Her heart was thumping, the flame of desire rising to engulf her until it seemed that only he mattered in the soft darkness.

Sara attended Mrs Grace who, as was so often the way with terminal cases, 'felt so much better this evening.' Afterwards, she drove back to Thatched Cottage. It was a clear, crisp night, with little blue mists floating over the burnished countryside. Now and then a rabbit scuttled in view of the headlights, and the fragrance of frosty earth and damp leaves wafted through the partially open car window. The atmosphere, suddenly and sharply, awakened an emotion both physical and elusively mental, as thoughts of Gavin crept insidiously into her mind, making him part of the night's enchantment. She scoffed at her reactions. What did a kiss represent, when based solely on desire and propinquity?

A few moments later she went into the cottage and stood on the threshold of the drawing-room, deliberately adopting a nonchalant air, but Kate cried, 'You look particularly happy tonight!' And as Kate spoke, she took in the flushed cheeks, sparkling eyes, and parted lips, not at all deceived by Sara's feigned casualness.

'I love autumn,' Sara remarked swiftly. 'It has the beauty of sadness, somehow— like music in a minor key.' She gave a little half-apologetic laugh, 'Must be getting poetic!'

Kate was far too discreet to ask where

Sara had dined, but almost immediately Sara volunteered, 'I had dinner with Gavin...strange man. One minute aloof and abrupt, the next unexpectedly sympathetic and idealistic. Can't fathom him.'

'Do you want to?'

Sara hastened, 'Not really, but—'

'Better to be intrigued than bored,' Kate remarked sagely. 'Bachelor types are invariably elusive—that's how they avoid marriage!' She stopped, adding, 'Although a disastrous love affair can embitter a man and make him behave out of character.'

'A good point...' Sara rushed on, 'I'm going to have dinner with his brother, by the way!' She didn't want to enlarge on the subject of Gavin's past, or even to dwell on it herself.

'Keeping it in the family! I understand that Stewart Morland is very well thought of in Hay. Charming, too; but, of course, you've met him...I forgot! He hasn't lost much time in inviting you out.'

Sara felt a little thrill of satisfaction.

'Stewart is very forthright; you know where you are with him.'

'A swift judgment!'

Sara thought of Gavin's remark about her assessment of Stewart and exclaimed,

'Accurate, though. Amazing how different two brothers can be.'

Kate smiled inwardly, knowing how Sara disliked being baffled by any man.

'You will be able to make a detailed survey of them both...I wonder who'll be next in the queue?'

'Kate!'

'Well, you have collected a few scalps, dear niece! A compliment!'

'But I'm still free and intend to remain so. Marrying the first man who attracts you could spell disaster. Emotional experience—' Sara stopped, colour rushing to her cheeks, as she added hastily, 'Well, that is essential.'

'You don't have to convince me,' Kate exclaimed, wondering why Sara found it necessary to stress the point.

Sara went to bed a little later, undressing slowly and savouring the luxury of solitude without loneliness, re-living the moments in Gavin's arms as finally she got into bed, her body heating, her heart quickening its beat, as the memory of ecstasy surged over her, making her restless and unable to sleep. 'Dinner with Stewart,' she murmured almost aloud, to counteract desire. And a flash of excitement and anticipation touched her. Her mood changed to sober reflection. She had been right to come to Ledbury. Life seemed suddenly an adventure which she intended to enjoy whole-heartedly, without analysis or anxiety. Concentration upon one man would be folly at this stage. And satisfied with that somewhat irrational philosophy, she settled down, a little smile on her lips as she closed her eyes.

It was two days later when Gavin and Sara faced each other in Gavin's consulting room after morning surgery. His attitude was tinged with an easy friendliness as he asked, 'Any problems?' It was his usual opening gambit but, on this occasion, Sara felt herself thinking wholly of how attractive he looked in his immaculate grey suit, white shirt and blue tie. There was a fascination, she thought also, about meeting a man again after a romantic interlude that bordered on intimacy.

As though sensing her reflections, he looked directly into her eyes and held her gaze for a second in a look of awareness, before getting up restlessly from his chair.

Sara allowed emotion to slide into the safe channel of professionalism as she

said smoothly, 'There *was* a problem....
A Mrs Winley. Thirty-nine. A number
of symptoms. Palpitations, hands going
blue; general malaise. I examined her,
but could find nothing wrong. I shouldn't
judge her to be a hypochondriac, or given
to exaggeration.' Sara added with relief,
'Would you see her? You have an instinct
for diagnosis. I feel totally inadequate. I
liked the patient. She was honest, and said
that she'd seen another doctor while she
was staying with friends a few weeks ago.
He couldn't help her either, apparently. It
isn't tied up with anything gynaecological.
I went thoroughly into all that.'

Gavin listened intently and then said to
Sara's surprise. 'I hope it's not a forerunner
of rheumatoid arthritis.'

'Arthritis!'

'Rheumatoid can start in many ways.
The patient can be very ill.'

Sara's brows puckered. 'Then I must
have a blind spot; the possibility hadn't
even occurred to me.'

'*I'm* only guessing. It just so happens,
should I be proved right, that I had a
similar case just before you joined me,
and it was not until symptoms of swollen
joints, stiffness, set in, that the condition

was diagnosed. I hope history will not repeat itself.' His voice was serious and sympathetic.

Sara, studying him, thought how impossible it was really to fathom his character, but as a doctor he could not be faulted.

The private line rang and he picked up the receiver immediately. Then, 'Oh,' he exclaimed, surprised but not displeased.

Sara made a gesture, suggesting she would leave, but he waved an expressive hand to indicate that he wished her to remain. And while she did her best to ignore the conversation as she sat and gazed out of the window across the sun-rifted grounds, words echoed nevertheless as he said, 'This evening...' Curiously enough, the only name that came immediately to Sara's mind was Marion Howard, and she hated the fact that it filled her with suspicion and disquiet.

Gavin's voice dropped slightly as he added, 'I think it would be better. I'll ring you back around four...' There was an intimacy in the promise, emphasised by the way he added, 'I hope so, too.'

He replaced the receiver and looked

directly into Sara's eyes without betraying his feelings in the slightest, as he asked, 'Could you be on call after surgery this evening?' He hastened, 'I know—'

Sara interposed, 'I don't mind in the least changing rota.' It was his turn to be on duty that evening and she didn't want any apologies without explanations. 'Just so long as I can rely on being free on Saturday,' she finished with pleasant firmness.

'Of course.' He became expansive as he rushed on as though the arrangements had not been of any great import, 'I'm due at the Marchton operation at midday. I promised Irene Marchton I'd be there. I hope it's a case of fibroids. She desperately wants children and a hysterectomy could damage that marriage.' He spoke like a man grateful to have avoided question and answer. Patients were always a safe topic of conversation.

Sara said unexpectedly, 'For a bachelor, you are very concerned about protecting marriages.'

He took that with an unexpected smile, 'Because I've no intention of marrying myself doesn't mean that I am indifferent to the happiness of those already married!'

There was a note of whimsical tolerance in his voice.

'Fair enough,' she managed to say lightly. 'I've certainly heard many eulogies about your marriage-mending tactics!'

'Better a marriage mender than a marriage wrecker,' he laughed, his mood noticeably effervescent.

'That is the last role in which I should cast you.' Sara met his gaze, tension and emotion creeping back. The sudden silence was electric. 'Self-protection is the guardian of morality, after all.' She smiled a little cynically. 'The side-lines are invariably safe.'

Sadness crept into his eyes, changing the atmosphere dramatically.

'Thank you for agreeing to stand in this evening,' he said quietly. 'Now we'd better get to work.'

Sara felt deflated. It was impossible to know where one stood with this man. Yet why *should* he have told her the name of his caller, or enlightened her about his plans? The spike of jealousy touched her, but she managed to force a polite smile and hurried from the room.

It was while she was passing the open door of Mrs Reece's office a few minutes later that she heard Gavin's voice, its clear resonant tones audible as he said, 'And book me a table for two at River Manor this evening.'

'Kington?' There was a note of faint surprise in Mrs Reece's exclamation, but she added, 'For what time?'

'Eight,' came the swift reply.

Sara hurried from the house. She hadn't any knowledge of River Manor, but she knew that Kington was comparatively near Builth Wells.

CHAPTER THREE

Stewart arrived promptly at Thatched Cottage at seven the following Saturday. Sara greeted him, aware of his immaculate blue suit and white shirt, and the smile that hovered at the corners of his mobile mouth while his eyes unashamedly admired her. He kissed her hand with a gallant gesture and said, 'Even the moon is on our side—perfect night.'

A spark of excitement touched her. She was receptive to his mood and met it with carefree pleasure.

'The hunter's moon,' she said blithely, 'that almost turns night into day!'

Kate appeared in the hall as Stewart entered it, welcoming him, and thinking that he was not in the least like Gavin, while, nevertheless, being a very attractive man and obviously a more extrovert character.

'We have a mutual friend,' she said easily, 'Ruth Dexter.'

'Ah!' It was an enthusiastic sound. 'Yes; a splendid person. Enjoys life.'

'As you do,' Kate hazarded.

'Indeed.' His voice was enthusiastic. 'There is no virtue in making oneself miserable, although doing so is a hobby with some people!'

Sara asked herself swiftly if that was a gentle and overt criticism of Gavin? She thrust the thought aside. Why should it be? Gavin was certainly not miserable, merely a more serious type.

Kate laughed. 'One way of putting it...' She looked from face to face. 'Don't let me detain you...' She moved towards the stairs as she spoke. 'I'm late and must change. The Morris's party this evening,' she flashed at Sara, 'for the ancient citizens!'

67

Stewart said, as he and Sara left the cottage, 'I can understand your aunt and Ruth being friends—they have the same vitality.'

'Oh, yes, Kate thoroughly enjoys life, too.'

'You look beautiful in the moonlight,' Stewart said, looking down at her as they paused beside the car.

'Thank you.' Sara's voice was light, she accepted the compliment as being part of Stewart's technique, determined not to take him seriously, but to enjoy the freedom of flirtatious relaxation...*Flirtatious!* What else had her candlelit dinner with Gavin been? So why put Stewart in an entirely different category simply because he had an easy exhilarating manner?

'I was afraid in case Gavin might want to rearrange the work-load and you have to cancel this evening,' Stewart added as they settled in the car.

'I made it very clear that I was not going to be on call this evening,' Sara said firmly.

'Strange man, my brother.'

'I thought you appeared to have a special assessment of him by the way you spoke that evening.'

'Oh! Concerning his dedication to his work, and secrecy! True... Now, I'm going to take you to an Italian restaurant between here and Malvern, only just recently opened.'

They skirted the eastern side of the Malvern Hills which rose majestically against the moonlit sky, their slopes massed with trees now bearing the rich tints of autumn, and suddenly, ahead of them, the restaurant, Traveller's Rest, came into view, its lighted windows glowing in the darkness like a picture of an old-world scene. Lanterns swayed gently on either side of its heavy oak door, illuminating the sign that hung immediately overhead.

And when Stewart and Sara went inside, they seemed to walk into the past where oak panelling, monks' benches, and a large log fire whispered of yesterday. Luigi, the beaming proprietor, came forward to greet them. He knew Stewart and appraised Sara, who said, 'This is perfect.'

'Thank you, Madame.' There was pleasure in the welcoming voice.

He ushered them to a corner table and left to get the menu and wine list.

As Sara sat down on the red velvet cushions that adorned the monks' benches,

Stewart said, 'Your velvet dress is most attractive, and that sapphire blue suits you.' He looked into her eyes. 'I am very fond of velvet; it is both luxurious and sensuous. Thank heaven women have become more feminine during the past year or so. Jeans and men's sweaters are fine on a boat, or for hiking—neither of which appeals to me I might add!'

Sara cried on a note of outrage, 'Living at Hay, and you don't care for river sports!'

He laughed. 'Squash and tennis are quite sufficient exercise—in small doses... Ah, Luigi; now what can you recommend?'

They chose river trout, escalope of veal and an Italian wine. The fire burned fiercely, the flames curling into blue tongues, testimony of the frost outside. Conversation was bright, often bantering and humorous, then, when coffee was reached, Stewart said, 'You are bewitching, Sara! And your smile—'

She cut in, 'And you are adept at compliments. Methinks it is due to much practice!'

'Quite possibly,' he agreed frankly. 'I'm not the strong silent kind. I could never see anything wrong in telling a woman that she is beautiful to look at, and delightful to be with! Provided, of course, that one is genuine.'

Sara gave a little lilting laugh to suggest that he would be complimentary even if it were *not* genuine!

'Ah! You've been influenced by my dear brother,' Stewart said. 'His uncompromising attitude is much more impressive, but that doesn't give him the monopoly of sincerity.'

Sara didn't want to think about Gavin, and certainly not to discuss him.

'And your face has instantly become serious to prove my point,' Stewart persisted.

Sara protested vigorously, then finished with a smile, 'I will accept your compliments with appreciation in future.'

'So there is to *be* a future,' he commented significantly. 'Can I take heart from that remark?'

'You know what I mean.'

'I know what your words *implied*,' he corrected, 'but that is not quite the same thing!'

'And I feel too smugly well-fed to argue. To say nothing of this pleasant wine.'

'How do you like working for Gavin?'

The question held a note of seriousness, and came unexpectedly.

'I like it very much; he is a fine doctor.'

'The best,' came the immediate reply. Stewart paused and then asked, 'Does he ever talk about himself? His life?'

Sara's heart quickened in faint apprehension.

'Not really,' she replied, adding defensively, 'I'm his assistant, not his confidante.'

Stewart nodded, his attitude reflective. 'Has he ever mentioned a Marion Howard?'

Sara echoed the name, startled and surprised.

'I have met Mrs Howard, and her daughter, Becky.'

Stewart's eyebrows shot up. He looked amazed.

'*Met* her!' The words were uttered almost in disbelief.

'Yes, she and her daughter came to Tudor Court the other day.'

'Good lord!' There was no mistaking Stewart's astonishment.

'Why do you ask?'

'Curiosity, for which I apologise. I've no earthly right to probe, and quite possibly put you in an invidious position. My brother's affairs are no concern of mine.' Stewart's expression was guarded, his manner restrained.

A sensation of dismay touched Sara as she sat there, conscious of sudden tension in the atmosphere. Now it was she who wanted to do the questioning, but something in Stewart's manner forbade it. She said deliberately, 'I thought Mrs Howard was both attractive and unusual.' Did Stewart know her? she wondered.

Stewart made no comment, and immediately changed the subject. Sara was left with the feeling that he considered he had made a glaring *faux pas*. From her point of view it had merely highlighted the mystery surrounding Marion Howard. Nevertheless she respected Stewart's attitude and he went up in her estimation.

The rest of the evening passed with easy communication. Gavin's name did not recur and when they had drunk their last cup of coffee, Stewart said regretfully, 'We are the only couple left here...I suppose I must take you home.'

'Sunday tomorrow,' Sara said brightly. 'Although I'm on call.' The thought of Gavin rushed back. Was he seeing Marion Howard? And had he dined with *her* at River Manor the other evening? In any case it was his business. How naive could she be, to give importance to his kiss? The very idea was laughable, she decided, feeling an inconsistent wave of happiness because the evening with Stewart had been such a success, and she had found him everything one could wish for in a host and escort. Yet what could he have told her about Gavin's life? And why was there such an obvious gulf between the two brothers?

They eventually went out into the sapphire blue night where hill and countryside quivered in the silver light, the cold exhilarating air touching their cheeks refreshingly, so that they both breathed deeply and smiled into each other's eyes, their reactions identical.

Stewart took her hand in a carefree gesture as they walked towards his car. There he stopped and looked down at her, his expression suddenly grave, 'There's just one thing, Sara, that I feel I ought to warn you about—'

'*Warn* me?'

'Yes; Gavin could break your heart. He has a power over women.'

Sara felt that she was being thrust into a dark world where fear was a spectre. She gave a little nervous disbelieving laugh.

'My heart isn't available for breaking,' she tossed at him. 'I'm not some inexperienced child, Stewart, and where has your loyalty gone suddenly?'

'I'm not saying anything that I would not be prepared to say to Gavin's face,' came the firm reply.

Sara shot at him, 'And of course you are Sir Galahad!'

He laughed, an indulgent laugh. 'I don't profess anything—unless it is to be in love with living! I am concerned for you, that's all.'

Sara shivered as though a ghost had brushed past her.

'I'll accept your solicitude. But I, like you, am also in love with living.'

'Then we'll say no more.' He saw her into the car and moved to the driving seat.

When they stopped outside Thatched Cottage he turned to look at her.

'Thank you for making it such an enjoyable evening.'

'It's been wonderful,' she commented honestly.

He leaned forward and kissed her lightly on the lips.

'That will do until next time,' he

promised as he drew back. 'I'll ring you.'

'Not at Tudor Court,' she said.

'Very well.' He waited until she had opened the front door. 'Goodnight, Sara; you still look enchanting,' he added blithely.

Sara went into the house rather in a trance. She *had* enjoyed the evening; she had been happy in Stewart's company, but his words about Gavin disturbed her, no matter how she tried to dismiss them. *'Gavin could break your heart. He has a power over women.'* There was a terrifying sensation in the pit of her stomach because she felt that the warning was not lightly to be dismissed. A shadow fell across the evening. What was behind Stewart's ominous words? And his reference to Marion Howard?

Kate was not back and the house seemed empty. Why hadn't she invited Stewart in? Would he think her inhospitable? He was a charming companion; different from anyone she had previously known. One was entirely at ease with him, without losing the edge of excitement. His kiss had been flattering without any suggestion that he was taking her for granted. Her mood changed. Ridiculous to dwell on cautionary advice, despite the fact that Stewart's previous respect for Gavin's private life gave that same advice greater validity. But the sentence, *'a power over women,'* re-echoed because she had already proved it to be true, not only in her own case, but because it manifested itself even with his female patients, all of whom fluttered and crooned when discussing him.

The telephone rang, making her jump because she was so engrossed in her own thoughts.

Gavin's voice said, 'Thank God you're back.'

'Why?' Her heart quickened its beat.

'Could you meet me at the York house? The husband's had one of his drinking bouts and attacked his wife. As you know, they're friends of mine. She needs a woman's support while I deal with him.'

'I'll change and be over right away. Hill Top, isn't it?'

'Yes.' There was a moment's pause. 'Sorry to drag you out.'

'It's what I'm here for,' she commented in businesslike tone.

She put on navy slacks and a white cashmere jumper, reaching the York house in record time. Gavin let her in.

'I've only just arrived,' he said in greeting.

Ivor York was slumped in an armchair, breathing heavily. His wife, Jane, was lying on the sofa, a dark angry bruise and swelling on her right cheek and eye. Her mouth was also swollen and she was crying quietly to herself like a child in despair. The room was in disorder with small tables, overturned, glasses broken, and a flower vase lying on the floor.

'I'm so—so *ashamed,*' came the plaintive sound. 'So sorry...I was *frightened.*'

'I'll get you to bed,' Sara murmured sympathetically, 'and then see to your eye.'

Gavin examined it; the bruising was bad, but superficial. An ice pack was needed.

'Oh, Gavin,' Jane York whispered brokenly, 'what am I going to *do?*'

'We'll talk later. I'm going to get some coffee into Ivor...I've made coffee here before now.'

'Gavin...' It was a pleading sound.

'Yes.'

'I wish I didn't love him.' It was a touching confession.

Gavin patted her hand.

'I know,' he said. 'Don't worry; nothing

I can say to him will be half as bad as his contempt for himself.' Gavin's sigh was deep. It was almost a year since there'd been any violence. Ironically, the marriage, otherwise, was a happy one.

It was nearly one o'clock when finally Gavin saw a shocked, but sober, man to bed—a man humiliated by his own weakness, distraught at the sight of his wife, and desperate because he had failed himself yet again.

'Forgive me,' he pleaded, clutching Jane's hand as she lay in bed, propped up with pillows. A hunted, dejected expression was on his face. 'Forgive me,' he repeated, 'I'll never be able to forgive myself.'

'Oh, Ivor,' Jane murmured sadly, her bruised and cut lip making speech difficult. She didn't take her hand away, and the sudden silence was infinitely poignant. Her eye was purple and red, her whole face disfigured.

He went stumblingly into the adjoining dressing-room, sobs tearing at him as he reached the depths of degradation.

Jane looked from Gavin to Sara. 'Thank you...thank you both,' she whispered.

'I'll be round early in the morning,' Gavin promised.

'I shall be quite all right now.'

'I'm sure of that,' Gavin agreed, 'or I'd put you into a nursing home.'

'He will need me,' she said simply, and now it was the mother speaking of a beloved, but delinquent, child.

Once again Sara went out into the night. The juxtaposition of being with Gavin, after her evening with Stewart, seeming ironical.

'Thank you for all your help; the ice packs made all the difference. Thank God there's only superficial bruising around the eye. It looks worse than it is.'

Sara exclaimed, 'The whole thing just doesn't seem possible! It's incredible how women can love men who treat them like that.'

'It's even more incredible that he genuinely loves her, too!'

Sara flashed a look of scepticism. 'I'll have to take your word for that.'

'You must have come up against these cases before.'

'The real alcoholics—yes. But in hospital it is all so much more remote.'

They had reached their respective cars which were parked one behind the other. The houses around them were in darkness;

the world was asleep, and their senses sharpened on the silence, while emotion crept stealthily upon them like a soft breeze rustling in the trees. They stood looking into each other's eyes, moonlight pouring down upon them; the shadow of the house they had just left falling across the road like a giant etching.

'I certainly don't feel like sleep,' he said quietly. 'This is an anti-climax.'

Suddenly, unexpectedly, he exclaimed, 'I'm going over to Builth Wells at lunch time to see Marion Howard.' In some inexplicable way he made the admission sound like a confession. He waited for Sara's comment.

'It's as well to know where you could be contacted in any emergency,' she said, deliberately refraining from showing any personal interest, or making any other remark. 'Although Bates would doubtless have your telephone number.'

Gavin's gaze met hers and fell away. He was aware of her seeming indifference.

'I'll give you a ring, during the day,' he said. 'I don't know quite what my plans will be... Oh,' his voice was low, 'our Mrs Grace died this evening. I was there,' he added.

Sara looked, and felt, distressed. She would have preferred to be there herself.

'I'm sorry you had to go out, but glad her suffering is over...how is Mr Grace?'

'Stunned; shocked.' Gavin added, 'I've sedated him. The son and daughter-in-law have arrived from Singapore.'

Sara looked at the house they had left. She didn't need to put her thoughts into words. The difference in the respective cases was only too apparent.

'Did you enjoy your evening with my brother?' The question came abruptly.

'Very much; very much indeed.'

Gavin nodded, and hastened, 'It's late and I'm keeping you out in the cold.'

Stewart's words rushed up at her, *'He'll break your heart.'* Just then desire was so overwhelming that she felt it wouldn't have mattered. Stewart was right. Gavin *had* a power over her, his presence bound up with a dark intensity, and a personality that exuded a mesmeric quality. He stood there invincible and challenging even in his solitude.

She shivered as she said swiftly, 'Goodnight...it *is* cold.' And before he hardly had time to move, she had opened the door of her car and slid into the driving seat, starting up the engine and racing away in a matter of seconds. She had, she told herself, ridiculed the idea of building up a kiss, but realised just then that it was impossible to forget being kissed by a man like Gavin, irrespective of romanticism or foolishness. She would liken the experience to a drug to which one could become addicted... The important thing, she finally decided, was to allow Stewart to provide an antidote...and thus be cured of the weakness.

It was a week later when Mrs Reece said to Sara on the intercom, 'Mrs Howard is here again, wanting to see Dr Morland. She hasn't an appointment, and I've told her we do not know when he'll be back, but she's asked to see you.'

'Me?' Sara sounded surprised and a strange sensation hit the pit of her stomach. 'Then I'd better see her,' she hastened. 'Bring her in Mrs Reece, and then make us some coffee. Dr Morland probably won't be long.'

'People should make appointments,' Mrs Reece said frostily. 'She hasn't her daughter with her, which is a good thing. Children can be so disruptive.'

Sara smiled to herself and waited for
Marion Howard, who came into the
consulting room as though quite at home,
greeting Sara with friendly naturalness, but
with a faintly apologetic air.

Sara was struck anew by her unusual
face, which might have been likened to
a rather lovely old-fashioned portrait. Her
expression had a quality of stillness, her
pallid complexion darkening her brown,
wide-set eyes which seemed to have lost
a little of their sadness. She wore a lace-
trimmed white blouse, and a black skirt
and cloak.

'Gavin isn't expecting me,' she began. 'I
ought not to interrupt like this, but now
that I'm here I do want to thank you for
being so kind to me and Becky when we
came here that day.'

Sara liked her. The word 'different'
applied, and Sara felt instinctively that
Gavin would be attracted to such a woman.
At that moment she looked very young, and
not at all like the sad widow of that first
encounter. But on the heels of that fair
assessment, a strange presentiment crept
over her, bringing back the initial fears that
Stewart had heightened. Obviously there
was some tie, some past link, between

this woman and Gavin. *A disastrous love affair…* that could encompass many vicissitudes. She, herself, might not want any serious relationship with Gavin but, woman-like, she shrank from his being involved with anyone else.

'Would you like some coffee?' Sara indicated the tray.

'Please.' Marion Howard looked around her. 'This is a very pleasant room—not a bit like a doctor's torture chamber! I'm sure you are responsible for all the feminine touches.'

'Gavin gave me a free hand.'

'Have you been with him long?'

'Since July.' Sara longed to ask how long *she* had known Gavin, but refrained from betraying curiosity.

Silence fell. The two women studied each other with perception.

At that moment the door opened and Gavin came into the room, stopping, obviously amazed to see Marion Howard sitting there. He had not spoken to Mrs Reece and was therefore unaware of her visit.

Sara reflected that it was impossible to judge whether he was pleased or annoyed by her presence.

'I'd no idea you were coming here today,' he said abruptly, adding swiftly, 'Is something wrong?'

'Nothing! I just had to come to tell you about the house.'

Sara was immediately alert. What house? The first reaction embraced the possibility that Marion Howard might be coming to Ledbury. Somehow it was the last thing Sara wanted.

Marion Howard rushed on, 'They've accepted my offer, Gavin. And I've got vacant possession in November.' She turned to Sara. 'I'm coming to Hereford to live—or about two miles out of Hereford. Only thirteen from here.'

Gavin said, and his manner was slightly awkward, 'I'm glad, since that's what you wanted.'

'And you liked it when we saw it on Sunday—didn't you?'

There was an uneasy silence.

'I liked it very much,' he agreed. Despite the praise, Sara felt that there was reservation in Gavin's attitude, and that the scene was somehow out of focus.

'I shall be almost on your doorstep, Dr Linford. I so hope we are going to be friends. Let's dispense with formality. I'm

Marion, and I know you're Sara.'

'Of course,' Sara exclaimed, somewhat abashed and aware of Gavin's seemingly formidable presence. It was the first time she had ever seen him at what appeared to be a disadvantage.

Suddenly Marion's attitude changed. She looked sad and moist eyed. 'Builth Wells is very beautiful, but it holds too many memories,' she said, her voice low. 'I want to get away—particularly before Christmas.'

There was something pale and infinitely pathetic about her.

'I can understand that,' Sara said sympathetically. Her gaze went to Gavin; he moved from one foot to the other, but did not speak. Why, she asked herself, since Builth Wells was only fifty-five miles away, had these two apparently lost touch, if his original greeting was anything to go by? And why, now the husband was dead, this sudden reunion unless there had been a past liaison? She felt tension building up and lowered her gaze, saying briskly, 'If you'll excuse me, I've a visit to do.'

Marion smiled. 'Next time I hope I shall be able to give *you* some coffee, or tea,' she said. 'Thank you, Sara, for not making me feel too much of a nuisance during your busy working day.'

When Sara reached the door, Gavin said, 'I'd like a word with you before surgery this evening. About the rheumatoid patient I've just visited.'

'Oh!' Sara was immediately interested. Mrs Winley was a favourite of hers.

When the door shut Marion said quietly, 'I know I ought not to have come here so impulsively. But I just had to tell you about the house.'

Gavin didn't contradict her, but said smoothly, 'Let's go into my consulting room. I have a few minutes before my next patient.' He led the way and settled at his desk, relaxing slightly.

'It isn't a matter of your not coming here,' he commented gently, 'but the fact that I cannot find the time to see people during practice hours.'

'Of course I understand...you *are* pleased about my getting the house?'

'Very pleased.'

'It being only thirteen miles from here will make all the difference...I've got to begin a new life, Gavin.'

'Yes,' he agreed solemnly.

'We can see each other...it was wonderful

to go to River Manor the other evening.'

'I thought you would like it.' He looked down at his desk and fingered the paper-knife. 'There's Becky to think of,' he said abruptly. 'You must make friends when you're settled. She needs the company of other children.'

They looked at each other. 'I know,' she murmured, and sighed.

The intercom went. Mrs Reece said his patient was waiting.

Marion reluctantly got to her feet, her gaze darting to Gavin's half-questioningly.

'I'll ring you,' he promised.

She nodded. He walked with her to the front door. No more was said between them. He looked grave as he returned to his consulting room. The past rushed up at him, leaving apprehension in its wake.

CHAPTER FOUR

It was a month later, after morning surgery, when Sara watched a somewhat hesitant patient come into the consulting room.

'Come and sit down, Mrs Knowles,' Sara said, indicating the armchair, then taking her own place at her desk.

Mrs Knowles was about thirty, dark-haired, olive-skinned, slim and expensively dressed. Her sable coat was luxurious and her shoes so soft that Sara suspected (rightly) that they could be bent from toe to heel. A subtle scent wafted sensuously.

She didn't waste any time as, peeling off her kid gloves, she squared her shoulders and, with a spurt of new-found courage, even defiance, said, 'I want to be sterilised, Dr Linford.' She gave a relieved sigh as if to say, 'And that's that.'

Sara uttered just one quiet word, 'Why?'

'I should have thought that's obvious!' There was a smile on Gillian Knowles' face. 'I don't want children; never have wanted them, and never shall. I'm happily married and my husband is wholly in agreement, so there are no snags whatsoever. I'm sick to death of the pill, which doesn't suit me...oh, and I've tried a good many varieties! IUD's send my periods haywire, and as for the rest of the contraceptives—they revolt me. Spermicides, caps...so you see I know what I'm talking about.'

'I'm sure you do; but how well do you know *yourself?*'

'Myself?' The tone was a trifle baffled.

'Yes, yourself. Sterilisation is a serious step, and we don't rush into the operation, simple though it may be. It could very easily be regretted by a woman who hasn't any children—or even if she has.'

A fierce resistant look spread over the attractive, faintly pouting face which was discreetly made up.

'I know all the questions and answers, Dr Linford. My husband might die, and I might marry again and then want children; we might get divorced and I might want to marry again and have them. My husband might come to regret it...it won't matter in the least what you say, or counsel, my mind is quite made up. And if you won't do it, then I'll find someone else who will.'

'I'm not a surgeon in any case, Mrs Knowles,' Sara pointed out.

'But Dr Morland is. He's both a surgeon and a physician, isn't he?'

'Yes, a surgeon on the gynaecological field. But he would say exactly what I am saying, I assure you.' Sara added, 'We only want what is best for our paitents.'

'And you're suggesting that I don't know what's best?'

'I'm sure that Mr Morland would need convincing, and wouldn't undertake to sterilise you unless he was quite satisfied it was the right thing to do.'

'I suppose you think I'm a selfish, unnatural woman?'

'No; some women are not cut out for motherhood. You may well be one of them, but I cannot accept the fact without going deeper into the matter.'

At that Gillian Knowles laughed openly.

'For a doctor you're very naïve. Do I *look* the type that would like sticky fingers jabbed in her face? Oh, I'm sure you mean well, and it is your duty to point out the snags. But this isn't any whim, I assure you. Nothing about child-bearing appeals to me—the whole business. My husband is all the family I want, and the reverse is equally true. And since he has to go to America on business early in the new year, we want the whole thing over and done with. He travels a great deal and I assure you that I'm never going to stay behind to look after a brood of screaming children. No way!' She flicked a dainty lace handkerchief from her expensive handbag as she spoke, fluttered it against her nose—symbolically like a determined child stamping its foot. 'I promise you that I shall have this operation done, and you are wasting your time giving me what you believe to be wise counselling.'

'Would your husband consider a vasectomy?' Sara spoke with quiet seriousness.

'He would; but I don't wish it. I've friends who have been sterilised, so I know what I'm talking about.' She added, 'There is something where they look into your tummy a—'

'Laparoscope Sterilisation; or there is the conventional surgical way with an incision in the abdomen. The fallopian tubes are divided.'

'Simple, I know,' came the confident reply.

'Quite; but I've not been talking about the physical aspects of the operation.'

'I know, and I hope I've convinced you.'

'How old are you, Mrs Knowles?'

'Thirty-two. I've been married for twelve years. If I'd wanted children, I've had plenty of time in which to have them.'

Sara smiled. 'With that I agree. I'd like

you to see Dr Morland.'

'By all means, since he's the surgeon. But I want to see him immediately—not for there to be any delaying tactics.'

Sara switched through to Mrs Reece and arranged an appointment with Gavin for the following morning.

'Eleven o'clock,' Sara said.

'Splendid...and you've been very kind. I do appreciate your point of view, and that you can't go sterilising people as though you were giving them 'flu jabs. I suppose there *are* some people who regret having it done.' She shook her head knowingly, 'But, believe me, I shall not be one of them! It will be champagne and caviare the day I can dispense with all this contraception lark. Spoils our sex life. And I felt like a turnip when I was on the pill! If my husband hadn't been mad about me, our marriage would have gone on the rocks, I assure you. And I may *sound* flippant, but this is a very serious matter to me.'

'May I ask why you haven't wanted to have this operation before now?'

'Simple; I didn't want the bother, and you must admit that it has become a very popular form of birth control these days.'

'It is also performed for health reasons; when another pregnancy would endanger the life of the mother, or—'

Gillian Knowles interrupted, 'I'm not concerned with other people's reasons, Dr Linford. My own are all I'm interested in!' She got to her feet as she spoke. 'I was prepared for your cross-examination and was a bit nervous when I came in to see you, but if it were possible, my resolve has hardened. Better a sterilisation than an abortion. And I shouldn't hesitate about the latter, by the way.'

Sara believed her.

'Until tomorrow at eleven.'

There was a little rush of scent, light footsteps crossing the room, and the pert little figure disappeared.

Gavin came in at that juncture.

'Who was the film-star I saw going out?'

Sara told him. And that he was seeing that 'film-star' tomorrow.

'She looked the picture of health.'

'Determined to be sterilised.' Sara shook her head. 'I couldn't shake her resolution.'

'U-m-m.' Gavin didn't seem surprised. Then as though he'd dismissed the incident, added, 'I've to go over to

Eastnor, by the way—to see Mrs Gillis and the baby.'

'Oh; they come out of hospital today... what time are you going?'

'After surgery this evening.'

Sara said spontaneously, 'Look in at Thatched Cottage and have a drink.' She hastened, 'You haven't seen my rooms yet.'

He didn't hesitate. 'I'd like to.'

Sara stood there a trifle shocked, wondering why she had obeyed the impulse to invite him. She also remembered that Kate would be out.

'I'll transfer the calls—would your aunt mind?' he hastened, half-apologetically.

'Not in the least and, in any case, I have a telephone in my bedroom so that Kate is not disturbed by any night calls.'

'Living with your aunt is still working well?'

'Couldn't be better.'

'I doubt if I can be with you before about eight-thirty... You know I'm to be godfather to the new son and heir, so I can't hurry away.'

'I'll expect you when I see you! The perfect cliché for a doctor!'

'We must all be a pain in the neck

96

where time is concerned,' he laughed. 'Always late.'

'It can become a habit,' she countered honestly. She thought of Marion at that second. Her name had not been mentioned for several days. It struck her suddenly that Gavin had been strangely preoccupied, and that this was the first conversation they'd had together since that afternoon.

He glanced at his watch and hurried to the door, where he stood for an imperceptible second, looked at her and said, 'Let's hope it's not a heavy surgery tonight, then we can get away at a reasonable hour.'

She nodded and smiled.

They got through surgery without any complications, and when they had finished Gavin said, 'I'll be off now. The sooner I get to the Gillis's the sooner I can be with you.' There was warmth and enthusiasm in his voice which surprised her, and awakened a little tremor of fear lest her invitation had been unwise. Then she argued that because she had been out with Stewart did not preclude her from offering Gavin hospitality. Colour dyed her cheeks. Why build up a drink into some big event having great significance?

Nevertheless, when she reached home that evening, she rearranged the flowers and looked around her critically to see if she could make any improvements. The sitting-room was small, but gave an illusion of space because it had two alcoves, partly used as bookshelves, on the top of which stood small lamps and delicate ornaments, giving colour and light. A pale mushroom carpet formed a perfect background for deep rose curtains and armchairs, while cushions of yellow and orchid lifted the scene, creating a soothing relaxed atmosphere. Leading from it was a bedroom of orchid and white, with an adjoining bathroom, forming an attractive suite. The padded satin headboard of the bed was decoration in itself, and hinted at luxury. Sara gazed at it all with a feeling of pride as she bathed and changed into a long pink velvet kaftan, braided at neck and sleeves. Her hair fell loosely about her face, and her dark eyes sparkled with the light of anticipation as she waited for Gavin's ring. The house was silent and empty. Kate had only daily help, and a cook who came as, and when, needed, her time divided between certain houses in the district. The clock ticked away; the softly shaded lamps glowing like illuminated roses to give a sensuous light.

Sara suddenly felt nervous and apprehensive. Would Gavin think it odd, being invited when Kate was out? Or would he not give it a thought? When at last the bell rang she jumped sufficiently to utter a little startled cry, and ran down the stairs, cheeks flushed, heart racing.

Gavin said as she opened the door, 'I'm earlier than I hoped.' He paused and took in the picture she presented. 'Even to a mere man that *is* a beautiful colour. And suits you perfectly,' he added.

'A very comfortable kaftan,' she said. 'Thank you.'

He glanced around him, anticipating Kate.

'My aunt is out,' Sara said. 'But we live completely independent lives, in any case, and neither intrudes on the other's privacy.'

'That's why it works so well,' he exclaimed without giving the fact of Kate's absence any significance . Having removed his overcoat he followed Sara upstairs, and once in the sitting-room, gazed about him in admiration. 'This is charming.'

'I must say I love it,' Sara admitted,

'and I have all my own books and ornaments around me. It is my home.' She made a little gesture. 'I have a bedroom and bathroom through there, so I am completely self-contained.'

They sat down and she indicated the drinks tray which stood on a small table by one of the alcoves. 'Whisky?' She hastened, 'Or brandy, since I don't doubt that you've already had some champagne!'

'One glass,' he admitted. 'Brandy would be ideal.'

'And for me,' Sara said. 'Would you—' She invited him to pour out the drinks which he did, and then returned to his chair settling deeply into it, and looking into her eyes as he took the first sip.

'Thank you for inviting me here,' he said, his voice deep, thrilling in its soft, yet strong, intonation. 'I've often wondered what your part of the house was like.'

'Really?' She looked amazed.

'You sound surprised. Is it so strange that I should be interested in someone who shares my professional life?'

'No, but—'

'What?' he demanded.

'It is very difficult to know what you feel, or think,' she said boldly.

Emotion flared as their eyes met and passion flowed between them.

'Can you repeat that at this moment?' he murmured hoarsely.

Sara felt that she was rushing towards a crisis over which she had no control. His attraction was almost menacing; his power absolute. And she had invited him there—impulsively, naïvely blind to the provocative implications.

She lowered her gaze and had a quick sip of brandy to give her courage as she tried to dismiss the hidden meaning in the question.

'One can never fathom the inscrutable,' she quipped, struggling against the excitement flooding over her.

'But one can recognise the obvious, Sara.' He added. 'If one so wishes.'

His gaze deepened and held her spellbound. She tried to escape, but was helpless.

'Yes,' she whispered, putting her glass down because she was shaking too violently to hold it.

The silence was like a spell, wiping out time and place as he reached her and lifted her from her chair, looking down into her eyes, his arms enfolding her, his mouth touching hers, at first gently and then with passion. There was a wild insatiable desire within them that made restraint impossible.

'I want you—desperately,' he murmured, his lips on her throat, his hands caressing her.

'And I, you,' she cried, lost to everything but her need of him. He began to remove her clothes, drawing her ever closer, until the hardness of his body awakened a frenzy, while they moved into the bedroom and finally lay together, desire like a fire engulfing them, lost to everything but the overwhelming need. As he pressed closer she yielded with a little cry, half pain, half ecstasy, which seemed to make even breathing impossible, so great was the upsurge of emotion in that last crescendo of fulfilment. There was no thought, no awareness of time or place, only the thrill of possessing, and being possessed; and when at last she lay still in his arms, the awareness of him beside her made her quiver with a sensation of utter abandonment and joy.

'Oh, *Sara*,' he whispered, his lips against her breast.

Her arms reached up and encircled his neck. Eyes met eyes in the wonder of revelation, and the gentle calm that follows in the wake of intimacy.

Neither needed words; this was a moment stolen from reality, which required neither analysis nor explanation, and Sara gave herself up to the experience with a yielding naturalness that enchanted him. They slept for an hour and, on awakening, were still held trance-like by each other's presence, and the wonder and mystery of the experience.

'I must leave you,' he murmured, still holding her.

'I know.'

'Don't move.' He spoke as though not wishing to break the spell. 'Go back to sleep.'

She didn't protest, just put her arms around him and drew him back to her for a second.

'Goodnight, my darling,' he whispered, and was gone.

She lay there, still in a state of ecstasy.

'He will break your heart...he has a power over women.'

Sara stretched luxuriously; she was utterly indifferent to the warnings in that moment.

Morning brought a strange suspended

feeling which made the ground seem unreal and the day part of a fantasy. She had slept with Gavin. Her first lover. *Gavin.*

Kate said, 'If you can come out of your trance long enough to take in a suggestion I have to make—'

Sara came back to reality with a jerk, smiled, met Kate's quizzical smile and said, 'I'm listening.'

'How about asking Gavin, Stewart and Ruth over for a meal one evening? Oh, I know Gavin and Stewart are not close, but their relationship might improve if they meet in congenial surroundings. I'd intended inviting Gavin in any case. You've made him sound very intriguing and I'm curious to know more about him.'

Sara couldn't resist saying, 'He came in for a drink last evening.'

'That fact doesn't preclude my inviting him to a meal,' Kate chuckled. 'He can bring a girl-friend if he likes,' she added wickedly.

Girl-friend! Sara felt very strange at the prospect, and the thought of Marion rushed back. Already the previous evening was taking on an element of fantasy. Had it really happened?

She said, 'Invite Gavin, by all means—' She stopped, colour mounting her cheeks. It was difficult to mention his name casually.

Kate gave her a shrewd look and a smile.

'I'll leave it until Christmas and make it a party. You'll probably think it a good idea to include Stewart, then. He'd be excellent at a party.' Kate glanced at the clock. 'Are you taking a holiday today?'

'Good heavens, no! Why?' Sara gasped. 'The *time!*' She got up from the table and grabbed her coat from the hall settle where she had put it in readiness.

'Don't land up in Malvern,' Kate called out comically. 'You work in Ledbury.'

The irony was, Sara thought, that her mind had been wholly occupied with memories of Gavin from the moment she awakened and she couldn't wait to see him! What would his attitude be? Why hadn't she said more to him? It was like being suspended between two worlds where nothing was real as she finally reached Tudor Court, looking in on Mrs Reece before going to open up the surgery.

'Dr Morland is out,' Mrs Reece said. 'He told me to tell you he rang you, but you'd just left. It's the Howard child. He said for you to cope with surgery and if there are any emergencies contact Dr Wood, who has been alerted.'

Sara's heart sank. The Howard child. This was the last complication she had foreseen and, from her own point of view, it couldn't have come on a worse day.

'Any idea of what's wrong?'

Mrs Reece didn't quite know why she, herself, was so put out, but she resented these friendly patients who dragged the doctor out, often on the slightest provocation.

'None.' She glanced at the clock. 'Better open up, Dr Linford, or they'll be banging on the doors, and it's a bitterly cold morning should anyone already be waiting.'

A bitterly cold morning.

Sara hadn't noticed that, either! But she had noticed Mrs Reece's somewhat dictatorial manner.

'We're not late, Mrs Reece...has something happened to upset you?' Sara spoke as one in command.

106

'Only that *friends* put upon Dr Morland. Thank goodness Mrs Howard has now moved to Hereford, or I suppose Doctor would have been dragged over to Builth Wells! All his appointments will have to be revised as it *is.*'

'Let me see the day book,' Sara said in businesslike tone. Given it, she mentioned three names familiar to her, and exclaimed, 'I'll attend to them, and you get on to Mr Graves and Mrs Dudley and see if they can change their appointments.'

Somewhat mollified, Mrs Reece calmed down, smiled half-apologetically and picked up the receiver.

Sara patted her shoulder and went through to surgery, aware that those patients who had counted on seeing Gavin would be disappointed, but consoled that her attention to detail and interest in their cases would compensate somewhat. One irate woman protested vigorously about 'people coming to the surgery blowing their noses, sneezing, and spreading their germs'.

'Don't worry,' Sara said reassuringly, 'people are infectious *before* they get the symptoms you describe.' But she knew, even as she uttered the words, that she was not believed and that the patient would stick to her own illusions no matter what she was told, or by whom!

Gavin rang just when surgery finished. A thrill went over Sara as she hard his voice.

'Sara?' His inflection held intimacy, and echoed significantly between them.

'I'm sorry about Becky,' she said.

'I've arranged for her to go into Emly Nursing Home.'

'Here, in Ledbury?' The words came jerkily and a feeling of dismay crept upon her.

'Yes; I can keep an eye on her. I've rung matron and arranged for a thorough investigation.'

'And Marion?'

'She's very upset, naturally, and is driving Becky over... And you?' he asked in a solicitous whisper.

'Fine...I've coped with surgery and manoeuvred your appointments.'

'I shan't be long, but don't tie me up any more than you can help this afternoon.' His voice dropped, 'I'd planned to take you to The Cottage in the Wood tonight, but—' he sighed, and added abruptly, 'we can talk later.'

Sara put the receiver down, her disappointment giving way to excitement. Gavin's manner was all she could have desired, his tone a caress, despite the circumstances.

The intercom went. Her appointment patient had arrived.

Gavin returned about an hour later. He looked anxious, but as he greeted Sara, murmured, 'This is the last thing I expected today.' He drew her gaze to his and looked deeply into her eyes as though they were re-living the ecstatic moments of the night before.

'How is Becky? What is the situation?' Sara's voice was unsteady.

'I don't like the look of her. There's evidence of bronchitis and possibly congestion at the base of the left lung; and she's running a temperature. They're doing a chest X-ray, blood count; throat swab. I'm thankful to have got her into Emly. Matron's splendid and the nursing care there is excellent. They'll let Marion stay, too. She's in a dreadful state.'

'I can imagine.' Sara tried to overcome her prejudice; prejudice born of fear. Yet perhaps now Gavin would fill in the background of the relationship; confide in her. She hastened. 'To have lost her husband so recently, and now for the child to be ill—' Sara watched him carefully as she spoke, aware of the shadow that crossed his face and the way he lowered his gaze from hers.

'A child being ill,' he exclaimed on a note of desperation, 'always seems so much worse than an adult, and she's such a bright intelligent—' He broke off. Then, 'Ah well, we mustn't be defeatist. As we know, children are up like rockets and down like sticks, and have amazing powers of recovery. I'll go back to Emly later on, and Marion will keep in touch.'

Sara asked herself just why Gavin was so involved. Stewart's remarks and attitude heightened her feeling of suspicion, and although she struggled to escape from the destructive emotion, it built up inexorably, leaving her tense and apprehensive.

'A good thing they had moved to Hereford,' Sara said.

'My word, yes!' The reply was uttered with fervour. 'I was going to have a talk with you about the medical aspect. Marion wants you to be her doctor. She mentioned it only the other day.' He spoke at greater speed than usual, and with a slightly self-conscious air.

'But surely *you*—' Sara stopped.

'No,' he said firmly. 'No question of my looking after her. Becky, perhaps.'

He spoke as though the matter was settled.

Sara felt a pang of doubt and misgiving. Marion was the last person she wished to have on her list, even though she couldn't have said why, since she did not dislike her; it was merely an intuitive shrinking from becoming involved.

'I hope she will not need looking after,' she said hurriedly, 'or has she a history of ill-health?'

The question came involuntarily, but she did not regret it, and looked at him intently.

He hesitated for a second, took a step towards his desk, picked up a letter, and said too casually, 'Not as far as I know.'

The telephone rang and he answered it immediately.

'Marion! Well, how is she? Doing the tests...good. She *will* look tired and be breathless... Now you must get something to eat. We don't want you on our hands, too. Yes, just as soon as I can.'

He had only just replaced the receiver when the bell went again, and this time

Mrs Reece said that it was Dr Stewart for Dr Linford.

Gavin said, almost curtly, 'For you...my brother.'

Sara looked, and felt, confused. Stewart had ignored her request not to ring Tudor Court.

'You promised to telephone me this morning,' he began.

She had forgotten and he sensed the fact.

'Out of sight, out of mind,' he exclaimed with a belligerence unlike him.

'Busy,' she temporised. 'I'll ring tonight. No, I can't make any plans...I don't know what I'm doing, and shall be on call anyway...goodbye.' She replaced the receiver. 'I'm sorry for that interruption,' she murmured to Gavin. 'I have made it clear that I'm not to be rung here—and that goes for all my friends.'

'Stewart makes his own rules.'

'Don't we all?' A faint note of hauteur crept into her voice. She didn't want to be talking to Gavin about Marion and Stewart, and felt a little sick disappointment because of the turn of events. She hastened, because she didn't want the incident to turn into discord, 'I take it that you'd like me to be on call this evening?'

'Please, Sara.' He looked at her and sighed. 'We'll make up for it...one cannot foresee these things. Now I suppose I'd better begin my day's work.'

'You've Mrs Knowles to begin with.'

'Ah! The one who looks like a film-star...' He nodded and sighed. 'There's something so final about sterilisation.'

'She's a very determined lady,' Sara said. 'I shall be interested to know what you think.'

When Gillian Knowles and her husband finally left Tudor Court, Sara went into Gavin's consulting room and said, 'Well?'

'You were quite right. Nothing, and no one, would dissuade her from that operation. After twelve years of marriage it is, from her point of view, the answer to all her problems. The husband was completely in agreement and, at the same time, quite prepared to have a vasectomy, but she wouldn't hear of that.'

'You'll do it?'

'Yes; she's had a good many trials and tribulations with all forms of birth control, and has an aversion to them, anyway.' He added, 'I'm convinced she would never allow herself to have any children...you agree with me?' He looked serious.

'Yes; I merely wanted to make sure—for her sake. I'm convinced that you are right.' She hastened, 'I've got a new patient coming any minute...what are you going to do for lunch?'

'What are you?'

'Coffee,' she said with a half-smile.

'I, too...I'll see you later on?'

It was a question asked with anxiety, and as Sara moved to the door he drew her to him and held her in a fierce grip as he lowered his lips to hers. Neither spoke as she drew away and went swiftly from the room, emotion swirling over her, his touch electrifying.

The rest of the day had a dreamlike quality, the only reality being the patients whose needs Sara catered for with instinctive precision and concern. There was no surgery that night, and when it was time to leave she said to Mrs Reece, 'Is Dr Morland with a patient?'

Mrs Reece looked up from her desk which she was meticulously tidying.

'Oh, no! He left for the nursing home ten minutes ago.' She added, 'Mrs Howard rang.' Mrs Reece got up as she spoke, putting the cover over her typewriter as though she were dressing a child. 'It's been a strange day. *Disorganised.*' She looked waspish. 'I suppose you are on call now?'

'Yes.'

Mrs Reece nodded, her wispy hair seeming to fluff out in disapproval.

'I thought you would be... Goodnight, Dr Linford.'

'Goodnight, Mrs Reece.'

Sara stood alone for a few seconds in the familiar office, listening to Mrs Reece's footsteps dying away. All was silent and filled with gloom, as though the building itself had absorbed the anxiety surrounding Becky's illness. The telephone alerted her in anticipation, and she picked up the receiver eagerly. Gavin might be ringing from Emly. But it was a wrong number. She sighed and went out into the darkness and damp of the November night. It didn't seem possible that life could change its mood so drastically in twenty-four hours.

When she reached Thatched Cottage, Kate appeared in the doorway of the drawing-room.

'Stewart is waiting to see you,' she said brightly, 'we're having a drink.'

115

CHAPTER FIVE

Sara felt guilty because she was in no mood even for Stewart whose company she had enjoyed on several occasions during the past weeks. He had been attentive, entertaining, flirtatious, but with an underlying note of seriousness on occasion. Once he had taken her over to Hay, showing her his attractive house (run by an elderly housekeeper) near the river, with views down its tree-lined banks. The practice quarters were completely detached, with an X-ray unit and all modern equipment.

Now, as Sara went into the drawing-room, she felt slightly self-conscious, as though her changed relationship with Gavin must be obvious to any discerning eye.

'I wasn't taking any chances,' Stewart said in greeting. 'Being on call doesn't preclude you from seeing your friends!'

His voice was without rancour, and his gaze appraised her. Sara realised that, when it came to it, she was pleased to see him. His attraction was indefinable but inescapable, and, as always, he lightened her spirits. Moping because she could not be with Gavin would serve no good purpose.

'Nevertheless I hope to be in for the rest of the evening,' Sara commented.

Kate said swiftly, 'Can you stay and have supper with us, Stewart?'

'I'd be delighted.'

'Then I'll see what I can find to eat,' Kate said breezily. She left them, puzzled by something indescribable in Sara's attitude and expression, even her manner.

'You've been very elusive this past week.' Stewart drew Sara's gaze to his in an inquiring, half-puzzled fashion.

Sara laughed. 'Just because I wasn't able to telephone this morning,' she countered. 'And how many more times must I ask you not to contact me at Tudor Court?'

Stewart gave her a whimsical look.

'I make my own rules,' he said.

Sara would like to have repeated Gavin's identical observation.

'And you *forgot* to ring, anyway. I knew by your voice, or was it that my brother's presence over-awed you so that you sounded uneasy? Gavin can be pretty daunting, I know.'

'Your first assumption was correct,' Sara admitted. 'We had a bit of a crisis—'

Stewart cut in, 'And I've heard *those* words before! You seem to have the monopoly of them!'

'This was different.' Sara felt that there was no reason to conceal the facts. 'Marion Howard's daughter, Becky, was taken ill and rushed to Emly Nursing Home.'

'Oh! I'm sorry. So they are obviously in the area,' Stewart said immediately.

'Yes; Mrs Howard has moved near Hereford.'

Stewart nodded. 'I rather imagined something like that would happen, seeing that she and Gavin were in contact again. Gavin will have his hands full.'

Sara tried to avoid the implication of Stewart's words.

'What is wrong?' Stewart asked sombrely.

'Until they get the X-rays and tests there isn't a specific diagnosis. Gavin spoke of bronchitis and possible congestion at the base of one lung.' As she sat there a cold sensation, half-faintness, half-sickness, washed over her. *'Seeing that she and Gavin were in contact again.'* Stewart's attitude was so positive, his acceptance without a trace of surprise.

In turn, Stewart was struck by Sara's emotional response; her uneasy expression which he felt was not wholly bound up with the child's illness, but rather by the fact of Gavin's association with Marion. Stewart knew, then, that his feelings for Sara were far deeper and more permanent that he had suspected, or, for that matter, ever intended. For the first time in his life he did not recoil from the word *marriage*, rather did he think of it as the height of his hopes and desires. Unexpected jealousy touched him as he wondered what ideas Gavin had about Sara, and how great his power and influence over her might be.

He said seriously, 'And Gavin still hasn't told you the truth about Marion?' He looked at Sara questioningly, almost with an air of interrogation.

Impatience mingled with Sara's apprehension.

'You asked me that before, and I'm still not—' She faltered, the memory of the previous night obliterating all else as she managed to add, 'I'm still not his confidante, and don't expect him to fill in all the details of his life's history!'

Stewart looked thoughtful, but there was a purposeful note in his voice as he said, 'Nevertheless I think you should know the truth now.'

'Why the change of attitude?' she retorted.

'Because of the change in circumstances. You see, Marion and he were once lovers. Marion and her husband, Nigel, eventually became reconciled for the sake of the child. Now that Nigel is dead there is nothing to stop them marrying. Marion would hardly have returned to his life unless that were the objective.'

Sara wanted to cry out; to protest, but to what purpose? *A disastrous love affair...* Defiance challenged the desperate hurt and pain that seared her as she cried, 'I do not see that this has anything to do with me.'

Stewart's reply chilled her with its logic and wisdom, 'Then if it hasn't, no harm will have been done by your knowing the truth: if it *has,* then you will be forewarned. Remember what I told you, that's all. I'm quite prepared to stand by the fact of having told you. And I pray that Becky recovers for both their sakes.'

And even as he spoke, Sara had the

disturbing feeling that he was withholding some vital fact.

Stewart leaned forward, his manner solicitous, 'God knows, Sara, I don't want to see you hurt.'

Emotion raged as Sara dwelt on the situation. Why, if Gavin had been in love with Marion, should he be so opposed to marrying? The answer sent a chill over her body. Marriage had deprived him of the woman he loved and, obviously, he had no interest in anyone else. His power over women, she thought bitterly, lay in his indifference to them, and through that indifference, the hurt he caused. The picture was stark and devastating. It also rang true. Could she deny that the characteristic by which she had been most attracted was his inscrutability? Thus, when he had made love to her, she had been mesmerised by the change of attitude, and the fact that he was the last person she would have expected to betray any interest. That first kiss had undermined her resistance and it was useless denying the fact.

She looked at Stewart with a sudden kindly calm.

'I appreciate your concern for me. But

half the time we hurt ourselves, and no one can protect us from our own folly.' She added, 'I am still not your brother's keeper...you, I take it, know Marion?'

'Oh, yes,' Stewart said slowly, 'I know her.'

'That sounds ominous.'

'It wasn't meant to. She just doesn't happen to be my type. Far too clinging, and wants protecting. The *femme fatale* causes much less upheaval...how about a day out on Sunday? Drive somewhere you like; have a meal—'

Sara hastened, 'I can't make plans just now. I must stand by.'

'Gavin can't live at the nursing home.'

'Marion is there with Becky.'

Stewart nodded and sighed, 'Of course; that means Gavin will be continually on call, as it were. For once I'm sorry for him.' He added, 'By the way, let Gavin know you've told me about Becky. I'd like news of her progress, so if you don't ring me I shall contact you—practice or no practice, if I cannot get you here.'

The evening dragged on and Sara heard, without absorbing, Kate's and Stewart's animated conversation, thankful when it was time to escape to her own rooms. She wanted to think, but could not come to any conclusions. So Gavin and Marion had been lovers—not an unusual situation and, she argued, not even Stewart could know the true facts of their respective reactions. The innermost secrets of the heart and mind were like a safe, of which only the individual knew the combination. Guesses were futile and she had no justification for righteous indignation because of Gavin's silence. He had in no way committed himself by way of promises, or even a hint of them. That, also, was true of her. They both had admitted to wanting their freedom, and she could not now rail at the premium likely to be paid for it. Should she ring the nursing home? But even as she was considering the possibility, her own telephone rang and she ran into the bedroom to answer it, hearing Gavin's voice with that upsurge of emotion that nothing could suppress.

'Sara? I thought you'd be anxious. I'm afraid it's scattered areas of bronchial pneumonia. She's on amoxicillin.' His voice was grave. 'The prognosis? Not easy to say... It's pathetic to see her.'

'And Marion?' Sara managed to mention the name as though its utterance was perfectly normal, but jealousy tore at her.

'Bearing up well; they're very good to her.'

'And you?' Sara asked in a low voice.

'Worried,' he admitted. 'Have you had any emergencies?'

'Not even a call...Stewart was at Thatched Cottage when I got home this evening, and Kate invited him to supper.'

'I see.' It was a clipped utterance.

'Will you be in for surgery in the morning?' Sara didn't want to discuss Stewart, or dwell on all he had said.

'Oh, yes...it's been a long day. I'm going home now.' He paused and then added with sudden unexpected passion, 'I can picture you...goodnight, darling.'

She replaced the receiver and sat there staring at the instrument. Last night she had been lying in his arms. Now she was sitting alone on the bed, her mind in turmoil, her heart aching and, contradictorily, rejoicing, at the same time. Was this the price of ecstasy that had been wildly snatched from life without thought of tomorrow? And now Marion had emerged from the shadows of suspicion, and stood in the fierce light of reality with its shattering truth. Sara got up and undressed, memory

124

rushing back, giving her body a new importance because Gavin had made love to her, his touch awakening rapture; his passion and gentleness opening up a new world. In some curious way she felt a different person, as though her identity had merged with his. What did she mean to him? In that moment she decided she didn't want to rationalise the situation, or indulge in any analysis that would confuse her. She had wanted him to make love to her, just as he had wanted to do so. Why should Marion's past relationship with him endanger the situation unless she, herself, allowed it to do so by indulging in foolish jealousy?

But nothing, she thought, when she saw him the following morning, was ever as simple as that. A look, and her heart raced; the sound of his voice thrilled her, even though he was talking about a patient. He had already been to the nursing home. Becky's condition was unchanged, but it was early days to hope for miracles. The amoxicillin had to be given time to work and the condition was, in any case, grave.

'Matron and the staff are being wonderful to Marion,' he said, a note of thankfulness in his voice. He added, 'One might say, protective. She looks almost as pale as Becky.'

Stewart's words, *'Clinging and wants protecting'*, came back again to Sara in a wave of fierce, near-resentment. And immediately she chided herself; a child's life was at stake; what did anything else matter? And she had no right to feel any grudge against Marion. Involuntarily, she said, 'I take it you have known Marion for some time?'

Gavin's expression gave no hint of his feelings as he replied, 'Quite a while, although we lost touch...now to work.' There was a briskness in his voice, and she felt that her question had cut through any intimacy that might have developed. 'By the way,' he added somewhat startingly, as Sara was about to go from the room, 'I wondered if you might like to look in at the nursing home this evening. Marion hasn't any friends in the district, and it's a lonely vigil. She likes you very much and would appreciate the gesture.'

Sara's eyes widened. 'Of course I'll go if you think it's a good idea...what about you?'

'I shall be around. We've Mrs Winley in

there; and Mr Cox. In fact it's very rarely Emly is without patients of ours, as you know! I have the freedom of the place!'

Sara forced a smile. The conversation had not progressed along the lines she had hoped, and she felt instinctively that the reference to the past had been the cause. Again Stewart's words echoed, *'Now that Nigel is dead there is nothing to stop them marrying.'* For a second all her common sense reactions to the situation vanished and the words struck a chill within her. The prospect haunted her.

'Is something wrong?' Gavin asked abruptly.

Sara hastened, 'No, why?'

'You looked very solemn—almost distressed.'

'Just the thought of dealing with Mrs Baker,' Sara managed to exclaim, thinking quickly.

Gavin laughed. 'Ah, the "if you don't tell me I'm ill, then you're a bad doctor" patient. You've spared me her list of symptoms, thank heaven.'

'Only this time when she telephoned, I didn't like the sound of some of them. Retention of urine and a complaint about indigestion. The ovaries could be suspect.

That's purely a snap—'

'And intuitive diagnosis,' he cut in. 'Strange how often one can be right.'

'Yes...I'd like you to go over her. This time her complaints sounded valid.'

'Then we can't afford to take any chances,' he said with conviction.

Sara sighed, knowing this to be true and wishing she had greater liking for Mrs Baker. Doctors endeavoured to treat every patient alike; prejudice of any kind strictly forbidden, but that did not mean a doctor was not human enough to prefer some people to others.

Stewart rang her just as she reached her consulting room.

'*Are* you going to be tied up this evening?' he asked, and she was aware of the anxiety in his voice, realising almost with a sense of shock, that his attitude was growing more serious. Honesty forced her to admit that she didn't want to lose his friendship. Firstly, because she genuinely liked him and, secondly, because, so far, he had created an atmosphere of carefree happiness.

'Yes; I'm going to see Marion and Becky.'

'Good lord, why?' He sounded surprised.

'Because I wish to,' she replied, feeling that explanation sufficed.

'How is she?' He sounded as though the question was an after-thought.

'Very ill. Scattered patches of broncho-pneumonia.'

He reacted immediately. 'Distressing; but she should pull through.'

'I've a patient waiting,' Sara told him. 'I'm sorry about this evening.'

'Are you, Sara?' It was a quiet, almost solemn question.

'Of course.' She felt a sudden apprehension. If only human relationships could stand still and keep within pleasant, comfortable bounds. She had no intention of ending her friendship with Stewart on account of Gavin. It was an out-in-the-open association which she valued and to which, she argued, she was entitled, having conveniently deceived herself until now that Stewart was not the type to get too serious, while being flatteringly attentive.

'Then let's make that date on the understanding that you can always cancel at the last minute. We've already mentioned Sunday. Lunch out somewhere?'

'The evening would be better,' she hastened. 'I might manage that.'

'Splendid.' His tone lifted.

'And if I have to put you off, you will understand?'

'Haven't I just said so?...I'll murder that brother of mine if you have to be on call!' He laughed as he spoke.

Sara was shocked when she saw Marion at Emly Nursing Home. She was hollow-eyed, pale and had a touching old-fashioned air, in her plain black dress with its neat, white lace collar, which seemed to emphasise her frailty.

'How is Becky?' Sara asked, her voice low. They were standing outside Becky's room in a gleaming white corridor which represented a world of mystery and illusion. The smell of antiseptics hung in the atmosphere—hygenic and spartan.

'Very ill.' Marion's eyes filled with tears. 'It will be a few days before the amoxicillin syrup begins to have effect... It's good of you to come. Everyone has been so kind. Gavin is here, but with a patient.' She opened the door as she spoke and ushered Sara into Becky's room.

Becky was propped up on the pillows, her face pale, her cheeks flushed. Her eyes were half-closed; she was breathless as well as restless and, Sara knew, a little delirious.

The small mouth was partly open, the lips dry. Sara choked and looked around her as a distraction to fight back the tears. There was no deceiving herself; Becky was indeed a very sick child. The subdued light of the room cast shadows upon the utilitarian furniture, and on top of the chest-of-drawers a few toys lay pathetically discarded. The table at the bottom of the bed had a little posy of flowers on it, but they looked on the point of wilting. The hush was deep and significant.

Becky's head, with its halo of dark hair, moved from side to side.

'Mummie—' The voice faded away.

'I'm here, darling.'

Gavin came in and automatically went to the chart at the bottom of the bed, studying it intently. Pulse 160 plus. Respiration 100–120. Temperature 103–104. He sighed and moved to the bed, studying Becky, his brow furrowed, his expression grave. Then he glanced at Sara and looked with anxiety and compassion at Marion.

'You must get some sleep tonight,' he said gently. 'And that's an order.'

Sara intercepted the intent gaze which implied that she would do as he asked because of their particular relationship. And once, Sara thought painfully, they had been lovers. The knowledge stabbed with the sharpness of a knife, and she tried to freeze her emotions because she could not endure further conjecture embracing the present. There was a light in Marion's eyes that pierced all the desperate anxiety; a light that illuminated her pale face, beautifying it. Sara knew then that the past was not dead and that it was only too obvious why Marion had moved to Hereford. Instinctively Sara's gaze went to Becky. Was it possible that she was *Gavin's child?* She thrust the thought aside as a treachery; a wicked flight of imagination stimulated by the drama of the circumstances and emotion over which she had no control. Every nerve in her body seemed frayed and tormented. Why think of such a thing? She took a deep breath, ashamed of the weakness. Yet was that conjecture the truth which Stewart had held back? There had been *something,* she knew.

When it was time to leave, she got up shakily, confused by what had seemed a nightmare.

Becky lay there helpless and suffering, and Sara wept for her. Everything was being done, but it didn't seem enough. 'Staff' came in with the quiet confidence inspired by nurses, as though their very presence could work miracles.

Marion would continue her vigil and as she, Sara, and Gavin stood outside in the corridor, he said, 'I shall be back later on.'

Marion put out a hand and touched his arm. 'Thank you,' she whispered poignantly.

Once having left the nursing home, Sara was thankful to breathe the frosty air and regain a semblance of normality.

'I've got to go back to Tudor Court to collect my bag and some packs,' she said as she and Gavin stood almost absent-mindedly in the car park. She hurried over the thought that she had conveniently 'forgotten' to put the equipment in the car.

'I'm glad,' Gavin said, looking down at her. 'A brandy wouldn't do either of us any harm.' He paused. 'What did you think of her?'

'A very sick child, I'm afraid.' Her voice was solemn.

He didn't speak, knowing she was right and that he was powerless.

'My car's over there,' Sara said, trying to keep her voice steady.

'I'll follow you.'

They arrived at Tudor Court within seconds of each other and went straight into the drawing-room. Gavin poured out their drinks in silence and they sank down into their respective chairs.

Sara couldn't blot out the previous night and the thought of it overwhelmed her.

As though by telepathy he said tensely, 'This is such a shattering anti-climax.'

Sara wanted to convey all that was in her mind, but she murmured softly, 'Yes, I know.' She hurried on so that she would not be overcome with emotion, 'And I'm standing by for the Price baby. I'd be happier if Mrs Price was in hospital, but there you are; I couldn't insist, or persuade, her.'

And all the time Sara was speaking, Gavin was looking at her, his gaze intense and caressing.

'You anticipate complications?'

'No; everything's normal, but the husband is the type who will want to call out the fire-brigade!'

They relaxed for a second, finished their drinks and Sara got up to leave.

'I hate your going,' he exclaimed in a low voice.

'And I hate going,' she admitted.

They both knew that these were not the circumstances in which she could stay, but he took her into his arms and pressed his lips to hers, firmly, passionately, and it was only with a super-human effort that she refrained from putting her arms around his neck and pressing close to him as emotion flooded over he inescapably.

'Goodnight, darling,' he whispered, and even as he spoke the telephone rang. He answered it immediately. 'Marion! I'll come straight over.'

Sara stood there, knowing that she loved him until it hurt.

Sara was up until late that night and finally delivered Mrs Price of a girl. As there were two boys already in the family, the delight was enormous. Champagne followed and an overjoyed mother played court for a very brief while before settling down to sleep, her world surrounded with happiness.

When Sara eventually returned home Kate, in a rich velvet house-coat, appeared in the hall.

'I thought you might like a hot drink,' she said in greeting...'did they have a girl?'

'Yes.' Sara flopped down in the nearest chair. She was physically and mentally exhausted and, like an anaesthetic wearing off, coming back to the reality of being in love with Gavin. It seemed like having salt rubbed into an open wound as she thought of him with Marion. 'Something sweet,' she said, never normally liking sweet things.

'Chocolate,' Kate said briskly. She didn't add that Sara looked as though she was about to become a patient. 'Get to bed and I'll bring it up to you.'

Sara didn't demur; she dragged herself upstairs, showered quickly, and was in bed when Kate joined her.

'Gavin rang,' Kate said quietly, handing Sara the chocolate. '*And* Stewart!' She hurried on, 'Gavin asked if you could come in early tomorrow morning.'

Sara felt that her love for him was written all over her face, but managed to say, 'And Stewart?'

'Just to have a word with you about Sunday.'

Sara sipped her chocolate.

136

'He's nuts; I only spoke to him about it today.'

Kate said dryly, 'He may be nuts, but he's falling in love with you, all the same.'

'Oh, Kate; don't be absurd.'

'Don't *you!*'

'I don't want any complications,' Sara groaned. 'Stewart's such good fun. I enjoy his company.'

'On your terms.' Kate studied Sara closely. 'You've skimmed over the surface of emotion so far—' She paused because she had been going to add, 'God help you when you really fall in love.' But something in Sara's expression stopped her and she added swiftly, 'But we all learn by experience...'

'Mostly, I believe, when it's too late,' Sara said solemnly.

'How's the little girl?' It was an abrupt question.

'Very ill.'

'Oh; I'm so sorry...it struck me that if all goes well, you might like to invite Mrs Howard and Becky—that's the name, isn't it?—here for Christmas. Gavin and Stewart, too. Ruth will come anyway.'

'Christmas!' Sara sighed deeply. 'I don't

even want to begin to think of it.'

'I do,' Kate said briskly with a broad smile. 'I'm old enough to behave like a child when you mention holly and tinsel... Have you finished your chocolate?'

'Yes, thank you...and thank you for being up. It's been one of those days.'

'I can see that...' Kate looked concerned. She took the cup and then pulled the duvet up to Sara's shoulders, and bent and kissed her forehead. 'Goodnight,' she said gently.

Sara smiled. 'You spoil me,' she murmured.

'It's lovely to have someone to spoil— that is if I did spoil you, which I don't!'

They smiled at each other. Kate turned out the bedside lamp and went quietly from the room.

Sara lay tensed, almost bewildered. She was in love with Gavin. It was a shattering realisation that seemed to create turmoil and devastation. He certainly was not in love with her; nor was he likely to be with Marion in the picture, she decided. How could she continue to work for, and with, him; to sustain their intimate relationship, when her heart cried out for his love, not merely the physical manifestation of it? So much for her desire for freedom. But her last thought before dropping off to sleep was that she could not bear to be without him.

Sara arrived at Tudor Court at eight o'clock the following morning. Bates said, 'Doctor is in his consulting room.' There was something ominous in his tone and Sara hurried to see Gavin. He was sitting at his desk, head bowed in his hands.

'Gavin?' Sara's voice was fearful and questioning.

He straightened himself and looked up.

'Becky died at four o'clock this morning.' His voice was hushed and sad. 'Respiratory failure...even an oxygen tent made no difference.'

'I'm so *sorry,*' Sara said, tears welling into her eyes.

'Marion's sedated,' he added, and there was wretchedness in the words which made Sara's heart sink.

'I'm so *sorry,*' she murmured again, with a feeling of dreadful inadequacy. 'If there's anything I can do?'

Gavin got up from his chair, restless, and at that moment indecisive. Then he said swiftly, 'If you could manage things here. I must take care of all the details...'

Sara choked. The expression on his face was bleak, shattered.

'I can cope here,' Sara said reassuringly. 'Don't worry.'

He looked at her with lingering tenderness. 'What should I do without you?'

A little spark of happiness touched her even in the grim circumstances. That Gavin, of all people, should admit to *needing* anyone.

'Will Marion stay at the nursing home?' she asked.

'I shall insist on her doing so at least until the funeral is over. She can't go back to an empty house. After all, she only has a daily, and there are limits to what any human being can suffer. Becky was her life.'

'We'll have to think of something,' Sara said. 'Things work out, Gavin. A platitude, I know; but true.'

He looked at her with an intent gaze. 'Amazing, isn't it? We deal with life and death every day, but when it hits home, it is all so different.'

'Hits *home*.' Sara's heart felt that it was bleeding. Wasn't it obvious by his attitude, and everything he said, that he was talking of his own child?

She just nodded, too emotional to speak.

'Hasn't Marion any friends here, or relatives that can be contacted?' The question came swiftly.

He squared his shoulders and a little of the grim inscrutable Gavin returned.

'None that she wishes to contact,' he replied shortly. 'Her life is very lonely.'

Why wouldn't he tell the truth? Sara asked herself. Why should he dissemble? Anger rose out of compassion, but she dare not voice her fears and said, 'You obviously know her life; I do not. I am just deeply sorry for her. I wish Christmas was not rushing upon us, because we cannot escape it, even if we want to, and that will make it ten times worse for her.'

'Christmas!' he gasped almost disbelievingly.

'Two weeks,' Sara said.

He stiffened and returned to his desk.

'She cannot be alone,' he exclaimed as though delivering an ultimatum,

In that second Sara felt that she had become a stranger and a lump rose in her throat as she struggled against unhappiness.

'We'll think of something,' she murmured.

He drew her gaze to his and the sad

conversation might not have taken place as he looked into her eyes, deeply, searchingly. He made a movement as if to join her, but Sara reached the door swiftly and looked back at him.

'Surgery waits for no man...we've got to take it.'

Gavin's voice was suddenly strong and disciplined. 'You are right. Open up. I'll be there.'

Almost involuntarily, Sara said, 'Do you think, Marion would like to come to stay at Thatched Cottage when she leaves the nursing home? I know I can speak for my aunt. Marion could spend Christmas with us—' She paused and watched him carefully, seeing relief spreading over his features as he said, 'But that would be a perfect solution. She likes you and she would be near.' He added, 'Are you sure?'

'Quite,' Sara said, her heart sinking because it was the last thing she wanted and yet could not bear Gavin to be faced with the problem of finding somewhere for Marion to stay. It struck her that she, herself, was plunging deeper and deeper into a situation that could only lead to trouble. *She* was going, in effect, to take care of the woman who obviously meant everything to Gavin; the woman he had loved, and probably still *loved*. Nevertheless the gesture had been spontaneous and genuine; how it turned out only the future would decide.

CHAPTER SIX

The frost of winter traced silver tendrils upon the bare trees, making them look like paintings on the canvas of the setting sun as it went down in gentle rivers of rose, purple and gold, as though the entire landscape was outlined against the sky, etching mountains of darkness in a blue sea.

Gavin said, as he and Sara returned from a miscarriage they had both attended, 'If we could have a day off before Christmas... Just *disappear*. I want to be with you, talk to you. There's been so much interference these past weeks that I've hardly seen you.'

Sara's heart quickened its beat; emotion swirled over her as she said, 'That would

143

be lovely, but impossible.'

'Why?' he asked.

'Because we can't both be away from the practice, and now that Marion is staying at the cottage I cannot disappear unless I have a good reason.'

'Marion is Kate's guest, and has no control over your actions.'

Sara longed to say, *'She has over yours,'* but thought better of it, not wanting to create dissension, or place him in an invidious position where he was forced to expose the facts. Until she, Sara, knew that his future was irrevocably bound up with Marion, she was not going to sacrifice the present for a possible lost cause. Meanwhile Marion had settled in with Kate as though they had been friends for years. Her grief at Becky's death was deep and poignant; her expression wan, as though life had been drained from her. All the same, it was noticeable that when Gavin visited the cottage she seemed revitalised, the sadness drifting away as she talked. Her dependence upon him was obvious, and his concern and readiness to help equally manifest.

Sara exclaimed, the words coming in a rush, 'By the way, I mentioned Becky to

Stewart. He was very sorry.'

Gavin started, his expression faintly apprehensive.

'You know he is spending Christmas Day with us?' Sara said.

'I assumed that would be so.' Gavin's voice was flat. 'You won't need any excuse to go out with *him,* I take it?' There was a touch of chagrin in Gavin's tone.

'I don't work for him,' Sara flashed back. 'The situation's quite different.'

'Yes,' Gavin agreed, sounding regretful.

'I hope Christmas will be as happy and peaceful as possible in the circumstances. At least we all know one another and shall not have to adapt to strangers.'

'Kate has been most generous,' Gavin said. 'I am more than grateful to her.' He lowered his gaze swiftly, realising that his attitude made it obvious that Marion was his responsibility, and that his objective was to protect her.

'Kate loves people and helping those in trouble. She makes sure they do not get morbid, either.'

'A very essential quality...nevertheless the arrangement for Marion was *your* idea.' He added, 'You're a very lovely person, Sara—and not just to look at.'

Sara flushed, made a little deprecating gesture, and said smilingly, 'Goodwill towards men.'

He put out his hand and clasped hers, emotion leaping between them; their need for each other deep and urgent.

Then, 'Damn!' he exclaimed, as the intercom went.

Sara dragged her hand away and went to the door.

'And you think we could escape for a *day?*' she teased.

'I'm determined that we shall escape,' he flashed at her, 'if only for a few hours.'

Sara felt that she was walking a few feet off the ground as she left him. In that moment she forgot Marion and even the sad problem of Becky. Conjecture was a dangerous pastime and she had nothing else with which to reinforce her supposition that Becky had been Gavin's child.

Christmas Day dawned, clear, frosty and bitterly cold. Thatched Cottage was the perfect setting for decorations which hung from its oak beams to give an old-world picture, enhanced by an enormous Christmas tree sparkling with tinsel and fairy-lights. A roaring log fire burned in the vast chimney-corner, glinting on brass and copper and offering a welcome to all who saw it. Marion had specially requested that none of the celebrations should be dampened because of her own sorrow, and she emphasised that since Becky, like all children, had loved Christmas, it would be as though she were there to watch the scene. Holly and mistletoe mingled with colourful garlands and lanterns; the mistletoe strategically placed so that full use could be made of it. Carols played softly, nostalgically, echoing from a music centre.

'It is so good of you to have me here,' Marion murmured, looking at Kate and Sara as they awaited the arrival of Stewart and Gavin. Ruth Dexter—staying over the holiday—looked thoroughly at home.

'We are delighted to have you,' Kate insisted. 'And we *understand*, don't forget.' As she spoke she looked at a somewhat battered teddy-bear which Becky had cherished and which Kate had suggested should sit at the base of the tree—to keep vigil as it were, and to establish the fact that Becky, after all, was with them...

'That is what makes it so—so special,' Marion whispered.

Gavin and Stewart arrived simultaneously,

Stewart coming into the house with a festive air, Gavin cheerful, but slightly more subdued. Stewart greeted Marion quietly, 'I was so sorry to hear of all this,' he said. 'It is a long time since we met. I know you don't want—'

She hastened, as they shook hands, 'Words hurt.'

He nodded. Everybody talked to everybody else, Ruth—extrovert, with a pink-and-white complexion and pure white hair—insinuating the right phrase at the right time.

Sara watched. Marion drew almost instinctively closer to Gavin as though he were an escort exclusively hers. Stewart studied them with faint amazement, unable to accept the fact that they were actually together. He positioned himself at Sara's side and said, 'Christmas would have been unthinkable without you. I'd had visions of abducting you for the holiday.'

Gavin overheard that, and without realising it, glared at his brother who lifted his head slightly and looked deliberately smug.

When the champagne was brought in, Kate beckoned to Gavin. 'Will you?' she said with a smile. She shot Sara a significant glance and quickly looked back to Gavin, who opened the bottle expertly as Kate surreptitiously slid another one into the ice-bucket.

Gavin's gaze met Sara's as they took their first sip; she might have been in his arms so great was the intimacy between them.

Stewart edged near to her, glancing at the mistletoe immediately above her head.

'A perfect position,' he said, putting his arms around her and pressing his lips against hers.

Sara drew back with a little startled gasp, laughing; but aware of the violent disapproval on Gavin's face as he remained menacingly still, his silence an indictment and testimony of his jealousy.

'I hear that you are living in Hereford,' Stewart said a few minutes later, addressing Marion, 'I hope when things are happier for you that we may all get together.'

Marion nodded, and Sara knew that she was mute because grief was welling to overwhelm her. The friendliness, the champagne, the warmth, snapped her control and the teddy-bear which had seemed a human touch, now suddenly became unendurable. Her lips trembled and she half-stifled a great tearing sob, which immediately brought Gavin to her side as, with an authoritative sweep of his arm, he guided her from the room. It was done so expertly that no one else noticed their disappearance, but Sara's heart felt like lead, the gaiety and excitement vanishing and giving way to a sick sensation of fear and disappointment. After a few moments she slipped away in search of them, unable to endure the suspense any longer. She reached the corridor leading to the study and heard voices, so that she stopped, almost holding her breath as she heard Marion say, 'I love you; nothing else matters now that I'm free.'

Sara froze, tense, fearful of being seen, her thoughts racing, her nerves shattered as she realized that no woman would make such an utterance unless involved in an intimate relationship; and while she, Sara, had not disbelieved Stewart's story, she had nevertheless, subconsciously, fought to minimise it. Relationships could be so distorted; even truth, itself, differ from actual fact. Jealousy spiked her heart as she thought of Becky...a man always had regard for the mother of his child, even after a divorce. At no matter what level, the tie between Gavin and Marion could only be great. Yet, despite this, even as she moved noiselessly away, Sara longed to be in his arms; her love for him intensifying rather than diminishing.

She returned to the drawing-room, champagne glass still in her hand, a smile on her face so that no comment was made about her brief absence.

But for her, there was no promise left in the hours that lay ahead; no magic in the fairy-lights and tinsel. She had some more champagne with a somewhat reckless defiance.

'What's happened to Gavin and Marion?' Stewart asked suspiciously.

'Marion was a little overcome by it all.'

'Ah, well; Gavin will look after her. It's strange seeing them together again. I hope Gavin knows what he's doing this time. He has a knack of conveying more than he means...I mean more than I convey,' he added quietly.

'And you are a past master,' Sara quipped, 'at saying charming things.'

'Only when I mean them.' He looked at her intently.

'Don't let's get serious today,' she warned sharply.

'It will have to come sometime, Sara.'

She lowered her gaze, then said firmly, 'I've never pretended, Stewart.'

'Nor I,' he insisted.

Sara realised with dismay that they had passed the light-hearted phase of their relationship.

'Ah!' Stewart exclaimed. 'Here they come...Marion seems all right now.'

I love you; nothing else matters now that I'm free.' What, Sara ached to know, had stimulated that remark? What had Gavin said to prompt it? And what had he said afterwards? But even as she reflected, she reminded herself of her previous appraisal of her own situation: she could not have it both ways; freedom had its penalties, and this was one of them.

Marion looked composed and smiled up into Gavin's face with a possessive little gesture full of confidence. He made no attempt to detach himself from her, and remained at her side, protective, considerate.

The Christmas meal was to be served at three-thirty. Open House had meant a succession of callers which was part of Kate's Christmas scene and, during a particularly noisy session, Gavin reached

Sara and murmured, 'Do you think we could manage to get out for a walk later on? That is, if you would like it?'

Sara, ignoring the scene she had witnessed a short while before, said, 'I'd love it!' She looked up at him. 'We can always take a torch!'

'You are all the illumination I need,' he whispered.

Stewart joined them at that moment, seeming very much the man in command. Sara escaped, not wanting to be involved in any discord.

Gavin said curtly, the moment he and Stewart were alone, 'Don't you imagine that—'

Stewart didn't allow Gavin to finish the sentence as he rapped out, 'You are in no position to tell *me* what to do. Just remember that. You've Marion to study—remember that, too.' He added, 'Having her here at all is a risky business, but that's your funeral! You never were very discreet.'

Gavin, grim-faced, turned on his heel and walked away.

Rain prevented any country walks that day; a day which became a matter of eating and lazing over the fire, fitful conversation, with always the awareness of Marion uppermost. After the morning breakdown, she succeeded in behaving normally so that when the gathering broke up, she had the satisfaction of not having dampened the festive spirit. Gavin and Stewart skilfully concealed their differences to behave in a thoroughly civilised manner, so that only Sara was conscious of the rift between them; a rift which Marion's advent had undoubtedly widened, possibly, she argued, because Stewart considered that Gavin was in honour bound to marry Marion, whether still in love with her or not.

Stewart said, addressing them all just before leaving the cottage that night, 'How do you feel about coming over to Hay for lunch tomorrow? No party, or anything like that,' he hastened, looking at Marion.

Gavin said with a quiet authority, 'Everyone is coming over to Tudor Court...you, of course,' he added, 'if—'

'Sorry, I'm on call, so I can't leave,' Stewart said. 'I can entertain, and slip out to the odd patient, but must be on the spot.'

Sara felt a wave of relief. The incident passed, and within a few minutes both men left.

Gavin surreptitiously clasped Sara's hand in parting, but not before Stewart had noticed the fact. He stepped forward and boldy kissed Sara on the cheek. 'That is in lieu of Boxing Day!'

When the front door finally closed, Sara's nerves were taut, and she was grateful the day was ended. She looked at Marion who was standing very still, a half-smile on her lips as she said, 'It will be nice to go to Tudor Court tomorrow...give you a rest, Kate.' Sara felt that the reference to Kate was an afterthought.

Ruth exclaimed irrelevantly, 'They're certainly two very attractive men. The only two bachelor doctors I've come across!'

'Then you haven't been in hospital!' Sara laughed.

'True; our family doctor has a beard and six children!'

Sara looked again at Marion. Thoughts rushed back. She, too, was in love with Gavin, and the fact seemed suddenly an affront that brought a deep sickening ache within her. But not dislike. For that Sara was thankful. Marion met her gaze slowly, reflectively; she might have been aware of Sara's feelings. It was as though the love they shared was a bond rather than a division.

Gavin looked at Sara and said fervently, 'Thank God it's all over!'

'Christmas, New Year?'

'Yes... Oh, forgive me, I wasn't thinking of the actual celebrations, so much as the general upheaval. I must be getting old, or into a rut, and I've missed you.'

She glowed. 'Since we've been together most of the time—'

'We've been *seeing* each other; not *together,*' he corrected. 'As I told you before, I mean to rectify that.' He stood in his consulting room, seeming more at home than in any drawing-room, a masterful expression on his face.

Sara's pulse quickened; excitement rushed up at her as she asked, 'How?'

'By taking you to The Cottage in the Wood next Tuesday,' he said firmly. 'Bates is going to see his sister for a couple of nights, so we can come back here and have a little peace, darling.'

He made the endearment a caress, his deep voice thrilling her, his purposefulness adding to the joy of anticipation.

156

'That sounds idyllic, but tempting providence!'

'Providence needs to be shaken up sometimes, or nothing ever happens in life. Frustration is poor company,' he added.

'So is grief,' she said, regretting the words the moment they were uttered. And as always, having said what she considered the wrong thing, she plunged deeper by adding, 'You and Marion have known that.'

He frowned, his expression darkening. 'I can't think of anyone who would not feel grief at the death of a child,' he said stiffly, the atmosphere changing instantly.

'I—I expressed myself badly,' Sara hastened, a tiny flame of anger rising within her because he had retreated from the truth. When it came to it, why should she apologise? But his attitude made her instantly vulnerable, conflict rushing back, the very name of Marion in association with him, awakening a previously dormant jealousy.

'I think we'd better leave it there, Sara...I'd like you to see a new patient. She doesn't like the idea of being examined by a man, so you will be prepared.' His voice was normal as he spoke, the dissension might not have taken place as he added with a wry smile, 'I always find such cases amazing in these days.'

Emotion surged back; that sudden awareness sharpened by the breath of anger. She wanted to rush to his arms, but instead left him without further comment, feeling nevertheless that a note of warning had been sounded which precluded her from bringing Marion into the conversation unless on an impersonal level. Yet wasn't that a contradiction, since Gavin had agreed to her, Sara, looking after Marion professionally? And how adamant he had been about not doing so himself...

When Tuesday arrived Sara could hardly believe in the excitement that surged upon her. Fear pursued her like a shadow lest anything should interfere with the evening. It was one of the worst months of the year for epidemics, and influenza was rife, the elderly invariably having complications that needed prompt attention and frequent visits. But when the moment came and she luxuriated in a scented bath before Gavin collected her—a colleague standing in so that every eventuality had been taken into account—she felt a sensation of overwhelming relief that the evening was theirs. She chose a simple, but elegant, golden-shaded cashmere dress, over which she wore a short sable jacket, and she knew when Gavin greeted her that he appreciated the choice. Their immediate desire for each other was reflected in a single look, and they went out to his car like two people walking in an enchanted world.

The sparkle of humour added to, rather than detracted from, their sensuality, as he said, 'Darling! We've made it! And I dare hardly look at you, I want you so much.'

She thrilled to his words, her glance telling him all he wanted to know. Her love for him seemed almost like another presence and she realised how difficult it would be to hide the fact, while conveying enthusiasm and excitement sufficient to sustain their relationship.

The Cottage in the Wood turned out to be a charming Georgian Dower House, standing in seven acres of natural woodland against the background of the Malvern Hills, with magnificent views across the Severn Plain, Evesham Vale, the Cotswolds and Bredon Hill. After a steady climb from Holywell Road, Malvern Wells, it came into sight like a miniature white castle, wooded slopes behind it, and gardens dropping away from a terrace at the entrance.

'It is perfect in spring and summer when the flowers are massed around it,' Gavin said, 'but even now it has a certain splendid elegance. I was determined to bring you here,' he added, as he manoeuvred into a convenient car park.

Sara was astonished by his remark. So! This visit had a continuity and significance.

They went into an attractive, carpeted cocktail bar, decorated in red, with comfortable seats and a welcoming atmosphere.

'No champagne cocktails...' Gavin said regretfully. 'Not since we are having wine, and I'm driving.' He ordered dry sherries. 'If we could only stay here,' he murmured after the drinks were served. He looked into her eyes as he raised his glass, and her gaze merged into his with the light of passion increasing.

'It is a very unusual hotel,' Sara said. 'Staying here would be like being in a lovely country house... *Have* you ever stayed here?'

'No.' His expression was thoughtful. 'With Ledbury so near, I have never considered the possibility until now.'

So, he had not been there with Marion! Sara discarded the name as though running away from danger. This was an evening to be stolen from time—not one of reflections or jealousies. Gavin looked handsome as he sat there, his immaculate suit and white shirt emphasising a glowing tan which was part of his complexion. His dark eyes lit up his face and mirrored every shade of expression and emotion.

A little later they wandered through the rooms, which were furnished with antiques wholly in keeping with the surroundings. Open fires burned in the grates; spacious sofas and deep armchairs, in delicate green, offered a maximum of comfort, together with a definite welcome. The dining-room in its glowing red, matching table-cloths, and candles, created a romantic atmosphere which made Sara say, as they were sampling the exquisite food, 'Thank you for bringing me here. This all reminds me of perfect wine—to be savoured...and even the wine we are drinking comes into that category.'

He said with a deep intensity, 'Being here like this...looking at you; *remembering...*'

161

Emotion flared between them, and they left a little later, as though reality vanished; and when they reached Tudor Court, a glance spoke for them as they went straight up to Gavin's room. There, he undressed her, pausing for a second to steal a kiss, and at last they felt the softness of linen sliding voluptuously to cover them and, with a surge of passion, found the warmth of body against body, lips against lips, arms clinging to draw them ever close, until they were one in mounting ecstasy, as desire reached that final explosive climax which brought cries of rapture from their lips. Identity disappeared, thought was suspended until, exhausted, they turned, passion spent.

Gavin kissed her tenderly, his limbs crossing hers, relaxed. No words seemed necessary and Sara felt that every muscle, every nerve, had been soothed and, like a child, she slept in his arms.

When they awakened, drowsily, it was one o'clock.

Sara stirred reluctantly and nuzzled her head on his shoulder. She wanted to stay, but knew it would be folly.

He held her fiercely and then drew back.

'I must take you home,' he said, his voice low and sighing.

'I ought to have had my car here,' she murmured, hating the stark mundane facts.

His kiss was hard and passionate before he swiftly moved from the bed. Sara followed, and as they dressed the spectre of parting made them both wretched. Sara wanted to cry out that she loved him, but feared to break the spell.

When eventually they reached the hall, he cupped her face in his hands and whispered, 'Sara...*Sara.*'

She looked up at him in wordless pleading before his lips crushed hers.

The moon was a golden circle in the sky as they reached Thatched Cottage. The light illuminated her face, giving it a radiance born of ecstasy and fulfilment. The dreamlike quality of the evening remained, mesmerising them. Their hands clung as she opened the front door.

'Goodnight, my darling,' he whispered, and then drove noiselessly away.

There was a message on the memo pad beside her bed. Kate had written:

Marion is not well but does not want to see the emergency doctor. Will you ring her when you get in?

Marion! Sara hated the intrusion which brought back the fears and suspicions. She had intended asking Gavin about the past, but when it came to it the evening had been too perfect for questions. With a deep sigh she picked up the receiver and dialled Marion's number.

CHAPTER SEVEN

When Sara got through there was a note of disapproval as Marion exclaimed, 'I've been waiting for hours for you to ring.'

'I'm sorry,' Sara apologised, 'but Dr Wright *has* been on call.'

'I don't want a stranger...and Gavin hasn't been available, either.'

Sara was not going to be drawn into any discussion and asked patiently, 'What's wrong, Marion?'

'My temperature's 102; I'm shivery and hot at the same time; my head thumps and

I ache all over. I feel really *ill.*'

'I'll come at once.'

She changed into her 'emergency' trousers and sweater, grabbed a suede jacket and went out into what she now realised was a bitterly cold night. With Gavin beside her, it could have been summer, she thought, struck by the irony of the situation. The roads were deserted, the countryside lying in a silver radiance as she reached her destination. The house, Wyvern, stood back in seclusion from a wide village green.

Marion, huddled in a thick quilted satin housecoat, opened the front door.

'You get straight back to bed,' Sara said with authority as she slipped off her coat and put it on a nearby settle.

Marion managed to do so, almost on point of fainting.

Sara made a thorough examination, but had no difficulty in diagnosing influenza. Returning her stethoscope to her bag and rinsing her thermometer in the adjoining bathroom, the thought raced through her mind that Gavin would be worried when he knew, particularly as Marion was alone.

'Mrs Brown, my daily helper, couldn't come in today, her son rang to say she had a bad cold.'

Sara said, 'Oh, dear...there's a chemist open all night in Hereford,' she went on, 'I'll go and get a prescription made up and bring it back immediately. Have you any oranges?'

'Yes...I'm so *thirsty.*'

Sara went downstairs, found a thermos jug, squeezed some oranges and swiftly returned with the refreshing drink which Marion sipped gratefully.

'Only liquids,' Sara admonished, 'not that you could face food.'

'You've been so good to me, Sara,' Marion murmured, 'not only just now...I'm so sorry to have dragged you out.'

'I'm so sorry you are feeling like this,' Sara said with genuine sympathy. 'But we'll soon have you better. You must stay where you are, and only get up to go to the bathroom.'

Marion nodded and, even in her feverish state, added, 'You smell nice—not a bit like a doctor!'

'We don't always bath in disinfectant!'

'You always look lovely.' The words came on a staccato note as she continued to shiver. She added anxiously, 'You will tell Gavin? And that I tried to get him?'

166

'Of course.' Had Marion hoped that Gavin would come over? Sara recalled Gavin's emphatic statement that he would not be involved medically. 'Now I'm going to the chemist.'

'An antibiotic?'

'Yes.'

'They upset me.'

'These shouldn't. You're not allergic to penicillin?'

'No.'

'I'll take the front-door key to save your having to let me in.'

'It's in the mortise lock...thank you. My head is *thumping*.'

'I know, and you're aching all over,' Sara said sympathetically. There was something infinitely pathetic about Marion as she lay there. A photograph of Becky stood on the bedside table, seeming to emphasise the loneliness and emptiness of the house. The bedroom was large and sombre, with heavy mahogany furniture that gave it an old-fashioned appearance. Patterned, dull red curtains did nothing to relieve the gloom.

I love you; nothing else matters now that I'm free.

The words seemed to echo harshly in

the silence, and Sara went quickly and noiselessly from the house; the sudden sickness in her heart unbearable; the thought of Gavin stabbing as she realised that it was only an hour or two ago that she had lain in his arms. How much longer could she bear the suspense and the secrets, rather than jeopardise a relationship that had an element of perfection about it? If only he *loved* her... She shut her mind against the destructive reflections. Time would inevitably answer all the questions, she told herself philosophically, not wanting to lose the sudden bubble of happiness that memory brought. Marion's condition might well precipitate a crisis, and at least she herself was not behaving like some embittered jealous woman! The credit did not, however, console her for long.

She raced to Hereford, got the Ampicillin, gave Marion the first dose, promising to keep in touch, then returned to Thatched Cottage where she snatched an hour's sleep before going to Tudor Court in order to prepare for surgery.

Gavin stole up on her as she was setting out the trolley, surreptitiously kissing the back of her neck.

She swung around to face him.

'Marion has 'flu,' she said without any preliminaries, watching his face and seeing the shadow that immediately crossed it.

''Flu...but—'

Sara explained. She noticed particularly that he made no protest about not being called. But she stressed that Marion had tried to get him.

'I'm sorry you were disturbed,' he said, adding significantly, 'you haven't had much sleep...' Their eyes met and they stood there, remembering.

A sudden unexpected and unfamiliar possessiveness surged over Sara. She loved him; they were lovers...surely that gave her at least the privilege of knowing *something* about his relationships with other women? Would he rush over to Wyvern? She resented the possibility, her mood contrary.

'What have you put her on?' Gavin asked, moving a few paces away.

'Ampicillin.' She added, 'I shall go over again later on.'

He said jerkily, 'I'll come with you...did she assume we were together last evening?'

'Should she have done? Or do you normally acquaint her with your movements?' The question came involuntarily, and somewhat abruptly.

There was an electric silence. His expression became grim, shocked.

'Had I already told her of my plans,' he said icily, 'I should hardly have asked if she assumed we were together. On second thoughts I'll see her in my own time... Thank you for all you've done.'

Sara was shattered by her own explosive feelings, as she exclaimed, 'You wanted me to be her doctor; that's why I didn't contact you.' She added, 'I seem to remember that you were very specific about not looking after her yourself.'

Gavin stood for a fraction of a second, withdrawn and aloof, then, without a word, went from the room.

Sara felt that she had experienced an emotional earthquake. Why had she allowed herself to lose control? To betray weakness she despised, and had thus far avoided? A sick, isolated and lonely sensation gnawed at the pit of her stomach. How could Marion's name fail to have significance from now on? Better deliberately to have asked questions in the first place, and risked the consequences. And she knew that nothing could lessen the ever-recurring fear that it was more than his relationship with Marion that haunted her;

it was the possibility of his being Becky's father that devastated her.

Professionally, it was one of those days when Gavin and Sara went their respective ways. Just before lunch Sara decided to go to Wyvern again, and contacted Gavin, having made sure from Mrs Reece that he was alone.

'I'm going to see Marion,' she said as she entered his consulting room. 'I'll be as quick as I can.'

He was sitting at his desk and glanced up from the letter he was writing. He looked very much the man in command; the man she had first met at the scene of the cardiac arrest case; the man who had said, *'I don't want to take on anyone who is thinking in terms of marriage...'* And her reply, *'I'm certainly not in search of a husband.'*

Her heart raced. And now she could not honestly repeat those words, because there was nothing in the world she craved more than to be his wife; to live with him; work with him, and be loved by him in return. Colour rose in her cheeks because it seemed that he must read her thoughts. But he said with quiet resolute politeness, 'Would you tell her that I will be in a little later? I haven't rung, in case she should be asleep.' He sighed, and continued in a professional tone, 'I don't like the idea of her being on her own.'

'We could get an agency nurse.'

'You will know more when you've seen her again.' He went on with solicitude, 'This coming so soon after Becky's death...her resistance is low and she's in a generally weak state.'

Sara agreed, feeling a numb misery, a wretchedness because it seemed as though she had suddenly been shut out of his life.

Gavin continued, 'Telephone me from there. I can have a word with her, then.'

'I'll do that.' Sara hesitated, wanting to say something personal, but he lowered his gaze and picked up his fountain-pen, beginning to write. Suddenly he looked up. 'I've just thought of Nurse Banbury.'

Sara echoed the name, mystified.

'She was on the staff at Emly and retired six months ago. She takes a few cases from time to time—to help people out. And she is willing to run the house, too. I'll get on to her—' he was already switching down the intercom and asking for Nurse Banbury's telephone number, which he dialled immediately.

Sara waited. It was obvious that Nurse Banbury was free and willing to take the case. She heard Gavin say, 'Mrs Howard is a very charming lady; lost her husband and small daughter within a year of each other. Needs taking care of, and you are good at that, as I well know. Exactly; a little bit more than just nursing... Immediately... I could run you over myself, this evening. Oh, of course; your having your car *would* be an asset. Then suppose we meet there? I'll try to make it as near seven-thirty as possible. Wait for me in the car.' He gave her the address and replaced the receiver, looking obviously relieved.

'You heard all that?' he said swiftly. 'Thank God for Nurse Banbury. Ideal person. Can't imagine why I didn't think of her earlier.'

'There won't have been much time lost,' Sara said.

'No...tell Marion that I've fixed it all up.' He appeared to be too absorbed with the idea to pay any attention to Sara. 'Tell her, too, that she'll like Nurse Banbury. Sympathetic, understanding woman.'

Sara stared at him. He met her gaze, but she knew that his thoughts were with

Marion who, now, would always be a shadow between them. And she, Sara, had prided herself on not behaving like a jealous woman! Now she felt that ugly word was her middle name.

Marion accepted the engagement of Nurse Banbury with thankfulness and relief. 'I knew Gavin would not let me be here alone,' she said with a confident sigh as Sara explained the facts. And when, after taking her temperature and pulse, Sara got through to Gavin, Marion lay there eager to talk to him, even though she felt so ill. Sara deliberately went downstairs to get fresh water and orange juice, returning a few minutes later to find Marion still in conversation. There was a little loving smile on Marion's flushed face as she said, 'Sara has just come back... The thought of this evening makes even my headache seem better. I felt sure you would find someone to look after me, and to *see* you...well...goodbye until later.' Her voice was low and sentimental. She replaced the receiver with a sigh, and looked at Sara, her expression a trifle sheepish. 'He's wonderful, isn't he?'

Sara smiled and set about clearing the

bedside table.

'And you've been wonderful, Sara...I'm not shivering quite so much; but I'm so *hot*.'

Sara busied herself making out a chart for the benefit of Nurse Banbury. Marion lay with her eyes closed. It was only when Sara was about to leave that she asked, 'When will you come again?'

'In the morning, unless Nurse Banbury needs me before then...but I don't think she will. This will take its course... What about a room for Nurse?'

'There's one next door. I kept it in readiness when Becky was ill. With central heating the bed is always aired.'

A devastating and, Sara knew, an unworthy thought, flashed through her mind: had Gavin ever stayed there? The possibility made her feel sick because it would smash every illusion she had struggled to foster.

She managed to say, 'Sleep all you can.'

'I'll try...thank you again. Tell Gavin not to worry.'

Sara felt a pang. Being an intermediary was not without a gentle irony. As she drove back to Ledbury it seemed that her whole world had changed and that a dark menacing shadow hung over the landscape.

When she reported to Gavin, he listened intently and said, 'Obviously she was making an effort when she spoke to me over the telephone...if her temperature doesn't rise this evening...'

'Unless Nurse Banbury sends for me, I shall not visit her again until tomorrow morning,' Sara said on a note of firmness. 'You will be seeing her, after all.'

'Not professionally,' came the swift comment.

'True,' Sara agreed, 'but you can hardly leave your professional *eye* at home.' She added 'Another drama over...I'm going to see Mrs Carson later on; she was due four days ago and I'm not going to induce her.' She searched for a glimmer on Gavin's face that went beyond mere professionalism, but none was forthcoming; he looked at her as a colleague, nothing more.

'We can afford to wait.'

'It's been a perfectly normal pregnancy. I took over from you, if you remember.' She hung on his reply.

'I remember,' he said. 'I thought she would be the ideal patient for you.'

'She has been, and has given me confidence, too.'

'That was the object of the exercise,' he pointed out. 'And you'd better go and get something to eat; with a midder in the offing, you cannot afford to miss a meal!' There was nothing in his manner to suggest annoyance, nor that he bore her a grudge for anything she had said; equally there was nothing to suggest the slightest intimacy, or an awareness of the previous night. His consideration was natural, and something that was an integral part of his character, no matter with whom he might be dealing.

'And have *you* eaten?' Sara wanted to stimulate some personal note.

'Yes,' he said briefly, and walked with her down the corridor. As she reached her consulting room door, the telephone rang. She answered it and said, 'I'll be over.'

She hurried to catch Gavin up as he was about to pass through to the private quarters.

'That was Mrs Carson's nurse, she said. 'Mrs Carson's started.'

'Another problem solved,' he said, with a friendly smile.

'I'll snatch a coffee.' She made the

remark deliberately. Would he suggest their having one together?

'A good idea,' he agreed, suddenly preoccupied. Then, 'I hope it will be a quick labour, so that you can take over while I go to Wyvern. Better keep in touch.'

Marion! Sara thought painfully. She had ruined the day.

Sara stayed for a glass of champagne after the birth of the Carson's son, and then went swiftly from the house. To have Gavin's child, she thought on the breath of ecstasy, memories rushing back.

Gavin was just seeing a patient out when Sara returned. He hurried to her consulting room, his expression anxious.

'Going to be a long—'

'No; it's all over. A boy, amid great rejoicing.'

'Oh, good!' He looked delighted.

'And I'm free to be on call this evening,' she said pointedly.

'Yes.' He didn't dissemble. 'Couldn't be better. Babies are not usually so considerate.'

Sara winced. 'They're a lovely family.'

'Ideal.'

'I had a glass of champagne.' She looked at him intently.

'Not a bad exchange for lunch,' he said.

Her eyes filled with tears and she busied herself with some papers on her desk. Didn't he even remember his remark about the champagne cocktails and the driving?

'I'm going to have a sandwich now.' She moved swiftly to the door. 'Mrs Reece said she'd see to them,' she added as she swung into the corridor.

'*Sara?*'

But she didn't hear him.

Stewart telephoned her at Thatched Cottage that evening. Would she have dinner with him?

'And I apologise for the short notice,' he added.

'I'm on call,' she said. 'Marion had 'flu and Gavin's gone over to Wyvern. He's managed to get a nurse.'

There was silence at the other end of the line.

'Stewart? Did you hear what I said?'

'I heard...I was just thinking how tied Gavin is, when it really comes to it. I suppose there's such a thing as being bound together by guilt, quite apart from anything else. In a way I'm sorry for him.'

Sara couldn't help saying shortly, 'I shouldn't be; I'm quite sure he likes the tie and the responsibility.'

'You're probably right...don't let's waste time talking about them...I've to go to Bourton-on-the Water on Sunday. I thought we might have a day out...it's a lovely spot and there's a splendid hotel at Lower Slaughter I'd like to take you to...' He paused.

Sara didn't hesitate in accepting and it was in no mood of chagrin that she did so. She enjoyed Stewart's company and it would be the height of folly, she told herself a trifle rebelliously, to build her life around Gavin, no matter how much she loved him. It wasn't merely pride; dignity came into it. She refused to dwell on all that Stewart had said at Christmas, or to take it seriously. She had been perfectly honest with him.

'Marvellous,' he said with enthusiasm. 'We'll finalise things on Friday. But, at risk of sounding like a gramophone record, see to it that Gavin doesn't spring any emergencies on you. With Marion ill, anything could happen. Thank God she has a nurse!'

'I will stake my claim tomorrow,' she promised.

'As I staked mine for a different claim at Christmas,' Stewart said softly. 'Don't deceive yourself, my beautiful Sara.'

His words were balm at that moment when her heart felt raw and her nerves were ragged.

'I don't *want* to do so,' she said honestly.

'Then I'll ring you on Friday.' His voice was contradictorily soothing and exciting.

As she got into bed that night, Sara thought that it had been a bizzare twenty-four hours, and she felt just then that she knew no more about Gavin's true feelings for her—apart from the purely sexual attraction—than on the day she first joined him.

Much to her surprise, Gavin telephoned her soon after nine that evening.

'I thought I'd let you know I was back and can take over the calls from now on,' he said.

Sara was genuinely relieved because of her need for sleep.

'Thank you...how did you find the patient?'

'Naturally, she feels pretty rotten, but when Nurse took her temperature it was down a point, which is a step in the right direction...Marion emphasised how good you had been.' He spoke appreciatively as he added, 'Your getting the Ampicillin so promptly will have made all the difference. And now Nurse is there, our immediate worries are over.'

Sara wanted to say, '*Your* worries, you mean. My concern is merely doctor-patient, with human sympathy thrown in!' But she commented, 'If only we could find nurses so conveniently for all our patients.'

Thee was a faint pause before he said, 'Get a goodnight's sleep, Sara.' His voice was gentle and solicitous.

'I will.'

Sara waited until after surgery the follow-ing evening before mentioning Sunday. The perfect opportunity came when he said, 'How about a small brandy? It's been a pretty heavy stint and we're long over our scheduled hours.'

'I'd like that...a good thing we neither of us have the clocking-in mentality.'

'Doctors wouldn't get far if they had,' he said with a wry smile.

They had hardly seen each other during the day and she looked for some sign of familiarity as they went into the drawing-room and he poured out their drinks, sitting down opposite her.

'Ah!' he said, 'that's better. Good to unwind.'

'Which reminds me,' she plunged, 'I'd like my day off on Sunday not to be changed, as it very often is—' She hurried on, 'I'm going with Stewart to Bourton-on-the-Water, and we want an early start.'

Gavin's expression became instantly grim.

'Stewart!' he said.

'He *is* a friend of mine,' she reminded him.

Gavin insisted with authority, 'I don't wish you to go out with him.'

'Meaning that you resent the friendship?'

'If you like to put it that way. But I'd rather we understood each other and—'

Sara exploded, 'I understand only too well, Gavin. It's perfectly all right for you to have a friendship with Marion, but I must not enjoy the same privilege with Stewart.'

Silence fell like silent thunder before he said, 'Marion doesn't come into this.'

'A very convenient philosophy,' Sara flashed. 'And why shouldn't she come into it? You can't have everything your own way.'

'It isn't a question of that,' he protested.

'I disagree; either there is honesty between us, or there isn't. You know all about my relationship with Stewart, but what do I know about your relationship with Marion?' The words tumbled out in the wake of anger, hurt and frustration. She ached for him to tell her the truth; to be trusted with the past, no matter what it might reveal in addition to that which Stewart had already told her. Just then she was fighting for their relationship, and to discover exactly what his feelings for her were.

She saw the dark annoyance on his face change to resistance.

'The nature of your friendship with Stewart is not in question,' he said sharply.

'Which gives you the advantage,' she said with a calm more impressive than anger. The thought of Becky crept back insidiously. How obvious it was that he had something to hide. She watched him, almost holding her breath in suspense as she waited for his comment, but his silence was like a wall between them, shutting her out, forbidding further discussion.

Finally, he said with quiet assurance, 'I will see to it that you are free on Sunday.'

It was like being dismissed; being told that, when it came to it, she had no real part in his life and that he had no intention of taking her into his confidence. She hadn't even the satisfaction of being flattered by his initial dislike of her friendship with Stewart. That was merely, she argued, because of family disharmony.

'Thank you,' she said icily, and got to her feet. It was impossible to stay there. She had slept with him in that room immediately above them; he had caressed every curve of her body, his touch gentle, yet passionately exciting. His lips on her breast had seemed to reach every nerve and sinew in ecstasy. Her gaze rested on him and she was fascinated by her own knowledge of his strength and power; the tautness of his limbs, the vice-like grip of his arms. It seemed that for a second they were each frozen to the spot as they stood, swamped by memories neither dare mention, nor even admit to remembering.

Politely, solemnly, Gavin saw her to the door and to her car.

'The roads will be bad,' he said quietly.

'I'm used to them,' she retorted. She drove away without saying goodnight, because sobs were choking her. She knew, then, that he didn't love her, and never would. Stewart's words, 'He will break your heart', echoed to haunt her.

With courage endemic, Sara refused to run away from Tudor Court after that dramatic confrontation with Gavin, even though she knew that nothing could be the same between them again. Marion recovered from 'flu, taking a considerable time to regain her strength, and beset by the depression all too often following on the infection. Sara gave her every care and attention, and while a holiday in the sun would have been beneficial, Marion refused to leave Wyvern and, Sara knew, Gavin. Every day, from Sara's point of view, was a test of survival, the transition painful as she managed to behave with friendliness that avoided any hint of intimacy. Gavin in no way challenged her attitude, nor introduced a familiar note. Marion came more and more into the picture and Sara accepted the fact that, after all, she had rightful priority.

Any personal matters between Gavin and Sara were invariably discussed after evening surgery, when they arranged the rota, choosing dates to their mutual advantage. On this occasion, Gavin asked, 'Any coffee?'

'Always coffee,' she said, going to the percolator which was forever in use in a small ante-room-cum-store-room, adjacent. For her it was a bitter-sweet moment. Now he would not follow her, or kiss the back of her neck, or even surreptitiously clasp her hand. It proved the theory, she thought sadly, of the psychologists who maintained that drastic changes in the pattern of human relationships were seldom, if ever, discussed, unless there was going to be a final parting. At least, she argued, Gavin didn't want her out of the picture.

He took the cup she brought him, and looked at her intently as though trying to assess her mood, her attitude; a faintly baffled expression on his face.

In turn she watched him, but all she saw was Marion. And she knew that she dreaded the months passing. It would not be long, she thought, before sufficient time had elapsed since Marion's husband died, so that she and Gavin could announce their marriage.

Suddenly, almost belligerently, Gavin asked, 'Are you going to marry Stewart?'

For a second she stared at him aghast, and then realised that, from his point of view, the question was valid. With a defiance born of anguish and frustration, she said, 'Quite possibly.'

He accepted her answer.

'So be it,' he said. His expression told her nothing of his feelings or reactions. He was like a man quietly assessing a situation and in no mood to reveal his judgment.

A voice called from the corridor, 'Gavin?'

'I'm here,' he replied.

Marion came gently into the room.

'Bates said I'd find you here and that surgery was over,' she said, smiling affectionately at Sara. There was nothing demanding or aggressive in her attitude, and she looked as Sara remembered her from the first day she arrived at Tudor Court. Unusual, devoid of make-up, with her large brown eyes, then more accustomed to sorrow than happiness. Now those eyes were soft and pansy-like; her whole attitude was receptive and hopeful. The dark misery had gone. 'You both never seem to stop work...is it all right for this evening?' She looked at Gavin.

'Quite,' he assured her. 'I was just snatching a cup of coffee.'

'And I must shut up shop,' Sara said, her heart feeling that it had received a blow.

Marion sighed. 'You certainly qualify for every job here, Sara. I really think you're wonderful...don't you, Gavin?'

There was no edge to the words; they had an innocence that made Sara ashamed of the jealousy she had, from time to time, endured.

The silence that fell was tense and full of emotion as Gavin said, 'I agree. I'm very particular about my colleagues.'

Sara made an excuse to leave them and went to her own consulting room. There she could no longer contain the utter misery and desperation she felt. The terrible inevitability of the situation surged over her, emphasising that the fight was irretrievably lost, and the last fugitive hope gone. Sitting at her desk she bowed her head in her hands and the tears ran unchecked down her face.

A voice said, *'Sara!'*

She struggled to conceal her emotion,

as Gavin stood beside her.

'What is it?' he asked urgently, 'What's wrong?'

She gulped, wiped her eyes and replied, 'Nothing; nothing, Gavin. We *have* been working at a pretty hectic pace.'

She wanted to run away; to escape from his powerful inquiring gaze which seemed to be looking far beyond her eyes and into her heart. For a moment she sat there, mesmerised by his fascination, and the doubting expression in his eyes. But she managed to give a little laugh as she got to her feet and said, 'You have enough crying women to deal with, without having one on your doorstep!'

'You are not a "crying woman",' he said significantly.

'No,' she agred, 'just a foolish one.'

Marion appeared, wanting, almost child-like, to see all that was going on.

Sara had recovered and was in command of herself.

'Don't forget,' she said to Gavin, 'that you have an early patient tomorrow. Mrs Reece asked me to remind you!'

Marion looked from face to face. 'What would you do without Sara?' she asked.

Gavin made no reply.

CHAPTER EIGHT

Sara lived through the weeks that followed hardly aware of her surroundings, or the events that took place. She might have been living in some isolated world where the only reality was the dull ache in her heart. She concentrated on work as a means of salvation, and if Gavin noticed her intensity of effort he made no mention of it. They worked in the same practice, were pleasant to each other, but completely detached when it came to personal matters. Her friendship with Stewart continued, and she found it balm which momentarily eased the pain to which she had grown accustomed.

And then one evening when they were having a drink together in her sitting room, he said directly, 'I told you at Christmas that we should have to get serious sometime, Sara.'

She knew it would have been foolish to ignore his words, or pretend she didn't understand them. She nodded her assent, allowing her gaze to rest on his with a trusting appreciation.

'You know I'm in love with you.' He was sitting opposite her in a deep armchair and now he leaned forward. 'Marry me, darling.'

The flamboyant light-hearted Stewart had vanished: he was earnest, slightly imploring.

Sara swallowed hard and took a deep breath. This was reality; the future. Nostalgia could only lead to a suffocating cage where the past strangled hopes and any kind of fulfilment. She needed protection against herself; protection from the thoughts and longings that were like her own shadow. To wallow in misery, and build up her love for a man who had no interest in her and was deeply involved with another woman was the worst form of nauseating self-pity she decided, as she said quietly, 'Yes; I will marry you.'

He looked surprised to the point of bewilderment, not expecting so ready an answer.

'Oh, Sara,' he murmured, and moved to sit beside her on the sofa, taking her in his arms and kissing her.

She allowed a little of the tension to drain

'Oh! To hell with Gavin,' came the blunt retort.

'All the same,' she said firmly.

He bent and kissed her lingeringly. 'If that is what you want, then autumn it shall be. We'll go somewhere warm for our honeymoon...'

'Yes.'

'What about your work?' He spoke seriously.

She said honestly, 'I'd be sorry to give it up, Stewart.'

'Then you can help me, if you would like to do so...but that can be settled later. I can't say that I shall enjoy the prospect of your continuing with Gavin, but you've a point about the time factor. We'll be fair.' He clasped her hand. 'What about telling Kate? Is she in?'

'Yes.'

Kate wasn't surprised so much as concerned. Recently Sara seemed to have lost some vital spark, and Kate had no evidence to support her theory that Gavin was to blame. She said, 'Bless you my children, and may you be very very happy.' She looked at Stewart and added, 'Sara's a very special person. Take good care of her.'

'You can rely on that,' he exclaimed stoutly.

'Then I shall have to arrange an engagement party,' she said brightly.

When Stewart was leaving, he looked somewhat solemnly into Sara's eyes as he said, 'I want to be with you when you tell Gavin that we're to be married.' He hastened, 'Pride, call it what you like! I shall not be exactly popular.'

'Why?' The word came abruptly.

'Taking away his highly successful colleague! Gavin doesn't like change.'

'And I don't like friction,' Sara announced, 'so no arguing!'

Stewart lightly discounted the likelihood. 'Of course not. He and Marion will be too involved with their own affairs to worry about us. I don't think he's ever considered the possibility of my settling down.' Stewart made a wry and faintly apologetic smile. 'You know how I mean that. We shall never "settle down" into that dreary rut-type marriage. Neither you, nor I, could take it, I'm sure.'

Sara commented brightly, 'No, relationships improve with a little variety.'

He kissed her, whispering, 'You're a wonderful person, Sara. And I'm the luckiest man in the world! I never thought I'd be making a speech like that to any woman!'

She didn't speak, just looked up at him, still bewildered by events and her own decision.

'I'll come over to Tudor Court after surgery tomorrow evening,' Stewart promised. 'Best time to catch Gavin and tell him, then you and I can go out to dinner somewhere.'

She agreed.

The following day was fraught with minor irritants. Patients, were late, difficult, and demanding. An accident case immediately outside the house brought a degree of chaos, since a young child was involved, and although in no way seriously hurt, the mother was convinced she was at death's door. Gavin was reassuring, patient and unruffled. 'One always has to allow for a parent's feelings,' he said to Sara after the superficial cuts and bruises had been attended to. 'One cannot rationalise them. And the shock doesn't help.'

Sara thought of Becky, and a wave of unhappiness surged over her. She couldn't stay the words, 'The little girl reminded me of Becky.'

A shadow crossed Gavin's face as she sighed and said quietly, 'That was in my mind, too.'

They looked at each other, but no more was said.

Stewart's arrival at Tudor Court that evening took Gavin by surprise when Bates announced his arrival. Gavin was in his consulting room after surgery, and Sara was hovering, trembling and apprehensive, dreading the ordeal ahead.

'Are you expecting my brother?' Gavin asked. 'Otherwise I cannot think what he wants, but, then, his movements are no concern of mine.'

'I knew he was coming,' she said.

'Ah...' The word was uttered significantly.

Stewart stood in the drawing-room, an air of confidence and undisguised happiness surrounding him, when Gavin and Sara joined him.

Gavin, inscrutable, self-possessed, moved to the drinks tray.

'Have you time for a sherry? A whisky?' he asked, addressing them in turn.

'Yes.' Stewart moved to stand close to Sara. 'But first of all we want to tell you that we are going to be married.'

Gavin let the stopper of the decanter go

down rather noisily before he turned, no flicker of emotion betraying itself, until he said smoothly, 'You will not expect me to show surprise... Every happiness, Sara. Congratulations, Stewart.'

Sara felt that her heart was lying like a painful lump in her chest. She sat down because her legs refused to support her.

'Thank you,' she murmured.

'So you're not surprised!' Stewart exclaimed. 'And I thought it would almost come as a shock!'

Gavin's expression was enigmatic, 'You underestimate me.' He raised his glass. 'To you both.' He turned deliberately to Sara. 'Does this mean you will be leaving the practice shortly?'

'No.' She hastened, 'That is—I mean, not unless you wish it. We're not being married until the autumn. I'd like you to find someone else before I go.'

There was no cynicism in Gavin's voice as he said 'That is very thoughtful of you.'

Was it a note of sadness that made the words curiously impressive, bringing a choking sensation to her throat?

'Sara wants to work with me,' Stewart said proudly. 'I'm a very lucky man.'

'Very lucky.' There was no hesitation in Gavin's agreement. His gaze met Sara's, 'I shall miss you.'

She fought back the tears, took a gulp of her sherry, and tried to think of some trivial thing which would stem the rush of emotion that threatened her control. It did not seem possible that she was sitting there, engaged to Stewart, behaving as though she and Gavin were friendly strangers. But that, she told herself fiercely, was life. Everyone met everyone else with whom they'd made love, and it meant nothing—nothing. Just an incident, forgotten, unimportant. Would *she* ever forget? Would she ever lose the desire for Gavin's kiss, for his arms about her? It struck her just then that physical pain could be borne with courage and fortitude, while love was a rasp that tore at the heart and offered no palliative. Without realising it, she looked at Gavin like someone wounded, and appealing for help, and gave a little empty laugh as she said, 'We all seem to hate change, particularly where our work is concerned.'

'And how is Marion?' Stewart asked conversationally. 'Recovering a little from Becky's death?'

'I don't think one recovers so much as

adjusts,' Gavin said solemnly. 'She has done that very well.'

Stewart nodded, finished his drink and said, looking at Sara, 'Well, darling—'

Sara got to her feet.

Gavin put down his glass with a gesture of finality. 'Thank you for giving me your news.'

'You're entitled to know who our future sister-in-law is going to be!' Stewart smiled. 'We must see more of each other and work up the family spirit,' he said in a conciliatory jocular fashion. 'I'm quite sure Sara will act as peace-maker.'

Gavin's gaze met Sara's and held it masterfully for a second, the silence heavy.

Stewart was oblivious of the tension as he moved towards the door, his hands outstretched to take Sara's.

'We'll keep you in the picture, Gavin,' he promised, his expression full of pride. 'We shall expect you and Marion to come to the engagement party.'

Gavin avoided Sara's glance. She didn't speak.

Once out of the house and in the car, Stewart said, 'You notice he never mentions Marion unless someone else brings her name up. Hope he won't let her down in the end. Strange chap. So reliable on the one hand, yet given to emotional extravaganzas on the other...I've been through hell with you working for him; always waiting for some complication or other...I could do no more than warn you,' he added, and gave a relieved sigh. 'Now here you are, all in one piece, and engaged to *me!* It's a miracle... You're very quiet, darling.'

Sara made a supreme effort, 'We can't both talk!' She laughed as she spoke.

'Gavin took your going quite well, I thought. No hint of any resentment or criticism.'

Sara said reflectively, 'I meant to tell him that of course I'd leave should he get someone suitable before the six months expire.'

'You'll have plenty of time to go into those details,' Stewart suggested indulgently.

She mentioned the position to Gavin a day or two later. It was a perfect May morning, when the garden was garlanded with blossom—lilacs, prunus, laburnum—all dripping from the branches like tinted snow cascading in a riot of colour against the deep blue sky, filling the air with a delicate subtle fragrance that mingled with apple-blossom—the orchards massed as though pink rose-buds had been crushed and blown to cling to the dark bark in a delicate unforgettable display. The beauty of it all hurt as Sara looked out from Gavin's consulting room, where she had been receiving instructions about a patient she was to see later in the day.

'There's just one thing that I forgot to mention the other evening,' she said. 'Obviously, if you should find someone suitable to take my place before the autumn, I shall understand and can leave at any time.'

'Thank you.' He looked at her long and speculatively, 'And *you* were the woman who had no intention of marrying,' he said without rancour.

Sara had forgotten her strong words; intent only on escaping from an unendurable misery in the belief that Stewart's love and need of her would open up a new horizon.

'Yesterday's folly,' she exclaimed.

The word 'folly' hung between them dangerously, her judgment shutting the door on any further discussion. Nevertheless Gavin continued to contemplate her with an unnerving scrutiny, as though intent on finding some chink in her armour, but she sat, hardly seeming to move a muscle as she said, 'As you know, Marion is coming to see me in a matter of minutes.' She got up and moved to the door.

Gavin nodded and hastened, 'I'll remember what you said about leaving. If I can find the right replacement, perhaps it would be better all round.'

'Yes.' Sara's hands were clenched. 'I could also ease her into the work, and save you the trouble.'

'Everything pleasant and civilised.' It was impossible to tell whether he was cynical, or rueful.

'Why not?' The modern jargon seemed apt at that moment.

Still he continued to study her, and she lowered her gaze before escaping into her own room. There she sat weakly, emotion tearing at her.'

Marion came in, subdued, almost tentative.

'I would like a thorough check-up,' she said, to Sara's surprise. 'I've not felt really well since I had 'flu and I get giddy sometimes. Not a very comfortable feeling when one is alone.' Her voice was flat, her eyes dull.

Sara made a thorough examination and as she pulled up the sheet, said, 'Your blood pressure is too high; that could well account for the giddiness. I can find no other reason for it, except that you are tense, stressed.' She added gently, 'Not even time can work miracles.'

Marion sighed. The ghost of Becky crept between them.

'No,' she agreed. Then, 'I'm so sorry, Sara; I haven't wished you happiness. Gavin told me about your engagement. I hope you will be very happy.' Her gaze was steady and speculative. She hurried on, 'The word "happy" is used so lightly that it often becomes meaningless.'

There was a sudden silence before she added, 'Gavin will miss you.' It was a firm decisive statement.

Sara turned away, busying herself with various instruments. 'It's a question of getting a satisfactory replacement,' she said, too casually.

'I should have thought it went much deeper than that,' Marion suggested. 'A question of knowing each others' methods, temperament...you're a fine doctor. I've told you that before, but it will not lose anything in the repetition. Will you go on working after you're married?'

Sara felt that she was discussing some imaginary character. There was no reality in the conversation, yet Marion seemed to give it earnestness.

'I shall probably work with Stewart... Now, you can get up and dress.' She smiled as she spoke. 'And I'll prescribe something to bring the blood pressure down.'

When Marion had dressed and returned to her chair in Sara's consulting room, Sara had the feeling that there was something a little strange about this visit; something that didn't quite ring true.

'You see,' Marion said, 'my blood pressure was high after Becky was born. They gave me Cetapres, but it didn't suit me.'

It struck Sara that Marion had never once mentioned her husband. The name never came up in conversation, as was normally the case. She also realised that she, herself, was forever trying to find reasons to discount even the possibility that Gavin was Becky's father. But what were

Gavin's feelings for Marion now? They had not been deep enough to prevent his being unfaithful to her, and yet he was obviously bound by too strong a tie to sever the relationship. Would he, even as Stewart had postulated, ultimately let her down? Was he in fact actually doing so, hence her stress and strain irrespective of Becky's death? A cold sick sensation washed over Sara as she looked at the woman sitting opposite her.

'If Cetapres didn't suit you,' Sara said, dragging her thoughts back to her task, 'then we'll try you with Inderal.'

Suddenly, almost vehemently, Marion cried, 'I must be well. I've *got* to be. It's vital.'

'Of course,' Sara agreed. 'I'll get the blood tests done and—'

'*You* don't think there's anything seriously wrong—do you?'

'I can find no evidence of it...you've been through a difficult time, Marion. Very often grief hits hardest just when people think they are well on the way to recovery.' Sara paused and added, 'After all, you lost your husband and—'

'That was different,' Marion cut in. 'I—' She stopped. 'Never mind. There's so *much.*' A fire seemed suddenly to burn in her dark eyes. 'But you'll help me; I know you will.'

'How do you like living at Wyvern, now that you've had time really to settle in?' Sara asked, introducing a less dramatic note.

'It's a gloomy house.' It was a flat statement. 'I bought it in too much of a hurry. I wanted to be nearer...oh, never mind.' She was twisting her handkerchief into a ball as she spoke, and there was near-desperation in her expression. Then, suddenly, her attitude changed as she studied Sara intently. '*You* look very weary,' she announced bluntly, 'and *you* haven't any problems!'

Was the remark, Sara asked herself, a way of changing the conversation which was edging towards dangerous ground? One thing was quite certain: Marion was under some great strain.

Sara said gently, 'If *you* have problems— any particular problems—might it not be a good idea to share them with your doctor?'

A rather sad wistful look came into Marion's eyes.

'You are working with Gavin,' came the

unexpected reply, as though the fact were self-explanatory.

Sara's heart quickened its beat. So this, too, involved Gavin.

'Everything you say to me is in confidence,' Sara assured her.

Again Marion's attitude changed as she brightened. 'Anyway, I haven't any secrets from Gavin,' she said irrelevantly. 'It is just that I don't want to be a nuisance...' She added swiftly, 'I wish I could tell you everything. There's so *much*—'

Sara dare not probe, or even prompt, although the temptation was overwhelming. She wrote out the prescription. 'Come back today week so that I can check your blood pressure. In the meantime, take things easily. Is Mrs Brown still coming each day?'

'Yes, thank goodness. I don't know what I'd do without her.'

'I'm not happy about your driving.'

Marion said immediately, 'My head gives me fair warning. It is as though I have a vice-like band tightening around it and I feel very strange. I *couldn't* go out, so don't worry.'

'Get the tablets and start on them straight away,' Sara said thoughtfully. 'Are you seeing Gavin now or—?'

'I'm having lunch with him here at one-thirty. I'll get the tablets first.'

Sara had the feeling that Marion was making a great effort to sound normal, but her eyes were suspiciously bright and her voice trembled. *'I wish I could tell you everything...there's so much.'* A weight seemed to be lying on Sara's chest, the suspense and tension unbearable. Lunch with Gavin...

'How is Kate?' Marion asked as she and Sara got to their feet, the consultation over.

'Fine.'

'Give her my love.' Marion looked long and appreciatively at Sara. 'You have both been so kind to me. I shall never forget.' She added, 'I hope life is very good to you, Sara.'

'Thank you...and don't worry, Marion. Oh, I'm not saying that in any general sense, but about your health. We'll get you right. I do understand, and remember what I said about driving. In any case, do as little as possible.'

'I won't...I wanted to make sure about the giddiness,' she said with emphasis, looking down at the prescription. She stooped forward and kissed Sara's cheek. 'I mustn't waste your time,' she said, 'I know how busy you are.'

Sara stood looking after her as she walked from the consulting room and down the corridor. There was a puzzled expression on Sara's face and anxiety in her eyes. She felt she had brushed the edge of the past, and been drawn inexorably into its shadow.

Gavin came out of Mrs Reece's office and, seeing Sara hovering in the doorway of her room, caught up with her, saying, 'Where's Marion?'

'She's just gone out to get a prescription made up.'

'Oh!'

'I want her to slow down, relax a little. I'm hardly breaking any confidences if I say that her blood pressure's too high.'

'How high?'

'175 over 104. I'm putting her on Inderal. She needs a real holiday, but it is useless my trying to persuade her to take one—not just now, anyway,' Sara added meaningfully.

Gavin looked uneasy. 'Wyvern hasn't been a success,' he volunteered... 'What are you doing for lunch?'

Sara felt that he wanted to change the subject.

'I'm having a sandwich and making Mrs Reece happy by doing some reports.'

'Over-worked,' he exclaimed, trying to sound bantering, but without succeeding, for his voice was flat.

'You'll have to emphasise that fact when replacing me,' she quipped, regretting the words as she saw the grim expression that immediately darkened his face.

'Nevertheless,' he said smoothly, 'I don't like your working through lunch...I expect Marion will have told you she is having lunch with me? Why not join us? I'm quite sure you are not behind with your reports.'

His invitation hung between them, and a wave of nostalgia swept over her as she said quietly, 'Thank you all the same. I really do have to catch up on the work.'

He looked down at her, accepting the excuse. Then he said unexpectedly, 'Talking of holidays reminds me that you are entitled to one.'

Sara managed to keep her voice steady as she said, 'My honeymoon will be all the holiday I need this year...what about you?' she stared him out.

'My plans are uncertain at the moment.'

'I thought they would be,' Sara commented. 'But don't forget that, with Norman's support, I could look after things in the event of your taking a break.' She forced a little laugh. 'That is, if you would trust me.'

His voice was deep and significant, 'I would trust you—you know that. You've become part of the practice—you know that, too.'

Marion came down the corridor and, seeing them, called out lightly, 'A consultation?'

'You got the prescription?' Sara asked absurdly, Gavin's words echoing to tear at her heart.

'Yes; they are very pleasant in that chemist's shop... Blood pressure,' she said to Gavin, making a face. 'I always associate it with dear old ladies and gentlemen.'

'Nonsense,' Gavin retorted.

'I don't really know much about medicine,' Marion said.

Sara didn't want to say anything that would inevitably lead to a reference to Becky. She said firmly, addressing Marion, 'Don't forget what I told you about driving.

As little as possible.'

'Doctor's orders,' Marion exclaimed, brightening a little. 'I love being told what to do by a doctor!' For a second there was radiance in her dark pansy eyes, and no mistaking the meaning of the look she gave Gavin.

Sara drifted away, leaving them together.

It was two weeks later, and a matter of days before the engagement party, when Sara was having an evening alone, catching up on all the neglected personal tasks, that she answered a ring at the doorbell to see Marion standing there.

'Marion!' Sara was instantly alarmed. 'Is something wrong?'

Marion was pale, obviously under great strain, but composed in a sad inevitable way.

'No, but I just couldn't leave without coming to say goodbye. You've been so good to me and I am so much better physically,' she added.

'Leave?' Sara's brows puckered. 'You mean you are going on holiday?' The prospect, no doubt involving Gavin, made Sara's heart race in apprehension.

'A long holiday,' Marion said solemnly. 'I'm going to America. For good.'

CHAPTER NINE

Sara heard Marion's words with shock and disbelief. There was only one word she felt capable of uttering as she said in amazement, 'Why?'

Marion walked with Sara into Kate's drawing-room, saying as she did so, 'Because I'm one of life's losers, Sara. I choose the wrong people. It is as simple as that.'

A desperate longing came to Sara in that moment—a longing to know the truth; either so that she might possibly retain a little respect for Gavin, or be able to despise him and thus free herself from his spell.

'I'm so *sorry*. I thought you were going to build a new life and—' She stopped, pained by the stricken expression on Marion's face.

'So did I,' came the heavy weary admission. 'But I'm not here to burden you with my follies. I've a hire car outside and I cannot stay...is Kate in? I wanted to say goodbye.'

Sara asked in bewilderment, 'But why didn't you give me some hint of your intentions? Why this sudden, dramatic change of plans?'

'It is only sudden in execution,' Marion said, 'not in planning. It was a possibility even when I came for that check up.' She sat very still for a moment, looking again like a painting—appealing, old-fashioned and hauntingly sad.

'I never dreamed—' Sara began and stopped as anger fired her because she knew that only one person was causing this suffering—Gavin. The facts, whatever they might be, would not alter that. His solicitude, his protection—all had been a sham. And Becky? What of her memory? Could he discount that, too? *One of life's losers. I choose the wrong people.* Could anything be more explicit?

Kate came into the room at that moment. 'I thought I heard voices... Why, *Marion!*' When told the facts, Kate cried, 'I'm so sorry, my dear. We'd looked forward to seeing you at the party.'

'I'm afraid I should have been very much the ghost at the feast,' Marion said and her voice hardened. 'And that's the last thing I'd want...' She seemed about to add something, and then stopped. 'I can only wish that life will be very kind to you, Sara. Unhappiness, loneliness—' She got up swiftly, her eyes filling with tears. 'You were both a tower of strength when Becky died.' She sighed. 'Who knows how different the pattern might have been had she lived...'

Neither Kate nor Sara spoke.

'I'm on my way to Heathrow,' Marion explained, 'and staying the night at The Excelsior so that I can get a morning flight.'

Sara was overwhelmed by apprehension. 'Do you know anyone in America? I mean—'

'I've a distant cousin who has wanted me to visit her... After that? Who knows?' There was a prophetic note in her voice. 'I'm selling Wyvern and everything in it.' She kissed them both in turn, thanked them again, and as she drove away seemed like a ghost lost in the night.

'Extraordinary,' Kate muttered as she and Sara went back into the house.

Sara sat down weakly in her chair. 'I can't quite believe it,' she murmured.

'Strange...I heard from Ruth that there was a rumour Wyvern was for sale. I didn't say anything because it seemed too far-fetched and, anyway, it is not in the district, so who could possibly have known?'

Sara's brows puckered. 'Who indeed?... Marion was so anxious to get the house, then found it gloomy. Small wonder after Becky's death. Something drastic must have happened for her to take this step, all the same,' she insisted.

Kate didn't mince matters. 'Something between her and Gavin, no doubt. He has been very much in the picture, after all.' There was a faintly belligerent note in Kate's voice. 'Be interesting to hear what he has to say about it.'

But to Sara's amazement, Gavin had very little to say when she mentioned Marion's visit to Thatched Cottage, and the fact of her leaving.

'I thought she would not go without saying goodbye to you and Kate.'

Sara gave him a rather bitter look.

'Her stay here hasn't contributed anything towards her happiness,' she commented somewhat aggressively; rushing on, 'and I don't somehow think it was all due to Becky's death.' The words were a challenge.

'You're probably right,' came the quiet non-committal reply.

Sara thought how strange human nature was. Now she wanted to defend Marion, plead her cause no matter what that cause might be, trying to ignore the fact that, now Marion was out of his life, he would again be free to pursue his emotional extravaganzas. His silence seemed to taunt her. Had guilt, the past, been responsible for the break-up of his and Marion's relationship? And what did it matter to her? What business was it of hers, after all? In two days' time her engagement to Stewart would be celebrated, her future secure.

'You will still come to the party,' she said abruptly and irrelevantly.

'Do you still wish me to come?' His gaze fixed hers and remained there unnervingly.

'Of course; you are Stewart's brother, no matter what happens. Family feuds are so juvenile anyway,' she added with a touch of scorn.

'Feuds are better than hypocrisy,' came the immediate reply. 'But I shall certainly come to the party. Believe me I want you to be happy, Sara.' His voice was low and gentle. 'Always remember that.'

'I shall be happy,' she assured him. 'I remember telling you once that Stewart made even saying "Hello" seem like a party. We have so much in common—our work, too.'

'I am aware of all that,' Gavin said gravely.

Emotion made Sara tremble. Again she realised how true it was that he could break hearts; inspire some wild untamable passion merely by a glance, a word. He seemed invincible at that moment, and no suffering he might have caused Marion could wipe out his influence, or lessen Sara's own desire. But with Stewart she would be safe, not because he professed to be a conventional down-to-earth type, but because he had the ability to make her laugh. Life with him would be exciting and never dull.

'And while we're talking of personal things,' Sara said with a quiet determination, 'if you *could* replace me before the autumn, I'd be grateful. I'd like a little time free from work before the wedding. In saying that, naturally I shall stay if you cannot find someone.'

Gavin met her gaze, his own steady and unflinching.

'Don't worry,' he said reassuringly, 'I already have a colleague in mind. You will have plenty of time to prepare for your wedding.'

It was not the reaction she had expected, but she managed to conceal her surprise.

'Thank you,' she murmured. 'I know you understand.'

'Perfectly.'

His manner told her nothing beyond the fact that he had no desire to prolong their association, otherwise he would not even be considering a new associate quite so quickly.

When she left him Sara realised that at no time had he betrayed his feelings, either about Marion's leaving, or her own departure. Had he forgotten that on one occasion he had said he would miss her, Sara? But that was yesterday, and yesterday seemed very far away.

Stewart was delighted when Sara told him of Gavin's plans.

'Gavin will never find it difficult to replace anyone,' he said. 'And in these days there are many people who would jump at the chance of joining his practice. I'm grateful he's being so co-operative. Did he enlarge on the Marion affair?'

'No, simply agreed with me when I suggested that I didn't think Marion's leaving was altogether the result of Becky's death.'

'You've got to hand it to him,' Stewart exclaimed grudgingly, 'he'd be perfect for MI5! And now to important things.' He felt in his pocket and pulled out a ring case. Can't have an engagement party without an engagement ring,' he said firmly. 'You said you wanted me to choose it; well, darling, I hope you will approve the choice—that's all.'

When Sara saw the ring she gasped, 'Oh, Stewart, it's *beautiful.*'

'It will look far more beautiful on your finger,' he insisted, slipping it into place.

A perfectly cut diamond, surrounded by smaller stones, flashed in the evening sun as they sat on the patio of Stewart's house. 'There seems something permanent about that,' he told her proudly. 'Oh, I know engagements are broken, but—' he shook his head confidently, 'ours won't be.' He leaned across from his chair and kissed her. 'I love you, Sara,' he said gently.

Sara held out her hand, watching the myriad colours flashing in the sun.

'I'm sorry that you had to wait a little while for it,' he said.

'It was worth waiting for,' Sara exclaimed.

'This had to be got for me and, as you know, adjusted to your size...it's a perfect fit.

'J and-a-half,' Sara smiled.

'Small,' he commented. 'You are quite perfect, Sara. Slim, just the right height. And that waisted dress, with the ruffle at the neck, suits you perfectly. Blue is certainly your colour.'

'Don't put me on any pedestal, Stewart,' Sara said forcefully. 'I don't profess to be perfect.'

'No, thank God,' he retorted with a laugh. 'And that makes two of us!'

They laughed together in harmony and understanding.

'I wish it were autumn,' Stewart said tensely, looking at her with unconscious appeal.

'It's June now,' she prompted. 'Three months—' She stopped, realising that it was the first time she had even sub-consciously thought in terms of an actual month.

'*September,*' he said with delight. 'I don't know why, but I had an idea you'd make it October.'

'September is a lovely golden month.' She looked at the wide expanse of the River Wye which flowed gently in the near distance below Hay Bridge. It was a peaceful tranquil scene, with its tree-lined banks. Soon she would be living there. She and Stewart would be able to explore the Black Mountains, and the upper reaches of the Wye, do all the things she had ever wanted. Travel, when Stewart could get away. She looked at him, hearing him say, on the day they first met, 'I'm sure you're finding my brother a very dedicated doctor. *Long hours; good to old ladies, but very secretive.*'

'Those were very deep thoughts,' Stewart teased.

'I was remembering the evening we first met, and what you said.'

'I remember warning you that you would see more of me.' He spoke with quiet confidence. The image of the pleasure-seeker receded.

'And marriage was furthest from your mind!'

'Yes,' he replied honestly, 'as we've said

before...I wish my parents were alive.'

'And I wish mine were alive, too...our children will be deprived of grandparents!'

Stewart took her hand. 'We shall have to make up for it.'

The light was beginning to fade and muted colours tinted the sky, reflecting the afterglow on the still waters in a soft rose hue that dyed trees and landscape. Sara tried to lose herself in the beauty of it all, to feel at peace, but all the time Gavin seemed to be watching, and her heart missed a beat at the thought of him. As she pictured him working with another woman, a sharp pang of jealousy stabbed her. Would he make love to that woman, also?

'I wonder who the colleague is—' Sara stopped, slightly embarrassed.

'Gavin's prospective candidate?' Stewart said immediately.

'Yes.'

'Obviously someone he knows. He certainly hasn't advertised, or the grapevine would have been alerted.' Stewart smiled. 'We shan't be told anything about her until she is actually installed—unless I'm very much mistaken,' he added significantly.

'Probably not,' Sara agreed, trying to

sound off-hand. She shivered at the thought of leaving Tudor Court.

'You're cold,' Stewart said with concern. 'And alas, I must take you home.' He clasped her hands and pulled her to her feet. 'Home will soon be *here,*' he said, indicating the white house that now faced them, a Paul Scarlet rose climbing beside the patio in a brilliant splash of colour. 'Life won't be so quiet as at Tudor Court. Gavin rarely entertains, and we don't associate with each others' friends. It was quite a shock when you appeared on the scene!'

They drove back to Eastnor in the radiance of the summer night; the sweet smell of honeysuckle and wild flowers filling the cool air with fragrance.

'I'll just ring you tomorrow,' Stewart said as they parted. 'You'll be busy with the party preparations!'

'There will only be a few people,' Sara said swiftly. 'I haven't really made any special friends.' It struck her, then, that her time had been entirely devoted to Gavin and the practice, and that she had been foolish thus to isolate herself. 'One or two patients are coming, and you don't seem to have swelled the list, either.'

'My particular friends happen to be on holiday...and you have yet to meet them. In any case the circle in Hay is more or less isolated from that in Ledbury.' He gave the point a certain emphasis.

Sara was grateful for the fact. Once she was married, she argued, she would lose touch with Gavin. Mutual friends could be a disadvantage, and she was thankful for their absence.

Thatched Cottage seemed to have become an extension of the garden on the evening of the party, for flowers were massed at every angle, throwing into relief the oak beams and wide chimney corner. Kate refused to admit the fact that she was striving to convince herself that Sara was happy, thus creating a world of make-believe.

Sara bathed and dressed with special care, wafting from the bathroom in a cloud of fragrance.

Her hair was taken off her face and coiled about her head, her skin flawless and delicately flushed. She chose a dress of blue chiffon, clinging and figure-revealing, the bodice fitting over her firm young breasts and unusually small waist. There was an allure about her, an elegance, that removed any suggestion of naivety while leaving her completely natural and unselfconscious.

When Stewart saw her he said softly, 'My darling, you look wonderful...in blue, too.'

'Thank you.' Sara smiled, appreciating his words and the fact that he was a demonstrative man, telling herself how fortunate she was, and that this was the evening most girls dreamed about, as they stood at the door of happiness, excitement and ecstasy.

Stewart made a fuss of Kate, complimenting her on the floral arrangements and thanking her for all the trouble she had taken generally, as he sauntered through the dining-room where a sumptuous buffet was arranged. Delicacies of every description—poultry, fish, meat and a variety of salads—represented an artistic achievement. Silver and cut-glass shimmered in the evening light.

Gavin arrived just as Sara was crossing the hall.

'I believe I've created a precedent,' he said in greeting.

'Really?' There was a question in the utterance.

'I'm early.' He added, 'Claiming the privilege of a future relative-by-marriage.'

The words lay between them with a significance that made Sara feel she was going down in a bumpy lift.

'Then welcome, future relative-by-marriage,' she said lightly.

'By the same token, may I say how attractive you look?'

Stewart overheard the remark as he joined them, and exclaimed, 'Praise indeed, coming from a true connoisseur.'

Sara felt that she was living on the edge of suspense, her own chaotic emotions isolating her in a world where she went through the formalities as the guests arrived, entering into their obvious pleasure at being there, and accepting their good wishes, genuinely touched. The one question that recurred was: 'You're not going to leave the practice, are you?' Her reply brought forth sincere murmurs of regret which made her feel that her eleven months at Tudor Court had, after all, been a success. If she hadn't made any close friends, she had at least acquired many grateful acquaintances.

Una Carson, whose son Sara had delivered only a matter of weeks previously, said ruefully, 'I shall seriously consider limiting my family to two, now! You made having Andrew almost fun... Oh,' she hurried on, 'that isn't any slur on Dr Morland; he's a wonderful person; it is just that I was able to tell you all my stupid reactions, and you understood.' Her smile was warm, even affectionate. 'I don't think women are ever quite so honest with a man, no matter how marvellous he may be.'

'Now I know,' her husband Daniel said. 'So *I* don't get honesty!'

'There are occasions when you'd be very surprised if you did,' Una Carson teased.

After the buffet meal had been eaten, the toasts drunk, Sara put on the music centre so that those who wished to do so could dance. The smooth lawns provided an ideal floor, and couples swayed rhythmically, delighted to be given the opportunity of enjoying themselves, free of formality and amid romantic surroundings. It was one of those perfect summer evenings when the intense heat of the day had given place to a warmth tempered by a soft fragrant breeze. Roses, massed in artistic little gardens, splashed their colour against larger flower-filled beds. Tall beech, poplar and weeping willow trees gave shade and, here and there, complete seclusion. A lily-pond shimmered, suggesting serenity, and completed the picture of perfect landscaping.

Mrs Reece, resplendent in navy taffeta, said to Ruth Dexter, indicating Stewart and Sara, 'Such an attractive couple, but Dr Sara will be sadly missed. She brought life to Tudor Court, opened all the windows as it were.' She looked at Ruth with owl-like wisdom, 'But Dr Morland will find it very different without her. Very different, no matter by whom she is replaced.' She nodded as she spoke.

And at that moment Gavin was saying to Sara, 'As this is a melody to which one can waltz...' He looked at her and took her in his arms. 'Your fiancé is dancing with Kate,' he added swiftly, as Sara glanced around.

Sara resisted any attempt to relax; conscious of his body touching hers, aware of him with an almost painful ecstasy, despising herself for the weakness and what she insisted was a sheer sexual fascination. As his arms tightened, she arched her back and drew away slightly, concentrating solely on conveying an indifference to his nearness, while drawing on thoughts of Marion to maintain control.

Gavin held her masterfully and they moved as one; she following blindly where he led, ultimately lost to her surroundings until he suddenly stopped and, without speaking, bent his lips to hers, parting them with a fierce possessiveness as he pressed closer, and felt the spasmodic yielding of her body against his in almost frenzied surrender, before she drew back, breathless, accusing, hostile.

'I'm engaged to your *brother,*' she cried with scornful condemnation.

'I am well aware of that,' he retorted coolly, his eyes dark and passionate.

'And my previous relationship with you is of no consequence or importance,' she went on fiercely. 'Stewart and I do not ask perfection of each other, but now he has my absolute fidelity. You,' she rushed on, her voice filled with anger, 'you think every woman is ready to—to—' She stumbled over the words.

'To—what, Sara?' There was indomitable strength in the question.

'And Marion,' Sara gasped. 'What misery did you cause her?' Having challenged him, she waited for his reaction.

But he remained icy calm, his gaze never once leaving her face as he said almost prophetically, 'All the words you can utter won't change the situation; you told me all I wanted to know.'

Stewart's voice came sharply from the near distance before he joined them, saying, 'Gavin, what is all this?' He took in Sara's flushed face and agitated manner.

'A slight difference of opinion,' Gavin retorted.

'Then,' Stewart rapped out, 'I suggest you choose a more appropriate time.' He reached out and drew Sara to his side in a protective movement.

Gavin gave him a withering look and walked away.

'What *was* that all about?' Stewart exclaimed.

'Nothing,' she murmured. 'I was argumentative.'

Stewart studied her in faint bewilderment, not wishing to force the issue, or upset her further.

'It's always a waste of time to attempt to argue with Gavin. In his own estimation he is always right.'

'I'll remember that,' she said with conviction. But she felt bleak and wretched.

Emotion had precipitated her into a dangerous mood of resistance, and she was acutely aware of the fact that Gavin had made no attempt to defend himself, or even to comment, when she had mentioned Marion.

'Friendship with Gavin never works for long, in any case,' Stewart said resignedly. 'It's always been the same. I'd rather liked the idea of establishing fresh ties, but when it comes to it...' Anger crept into his voice, 'I'm certainly not going to have you annoyed.' He looked down at her. 'Now let's go back to the party.'

Sara wondered if Gavin might have made some excuse and left, but when she and Stewart returned to the main lawn, Gavin was sitting with Una Carson on the cushioned hammock, drink in hand.

Dusk fell; the sunset fired the sky, its reflection giving a stereoscopic effect to every flower, shrub and tree. The light held a curious luminosity, beautifying, romantic, as the afterglow tinted the clouds, turning them into landscapes rising from an opal sea; the colours so delicate that they might have been painted by a magic brush. And still Gavin stayed, even when, an hour or two later, guests began to leave until, finally, he was the only one remaining, his manner almost dogged as Kate said, 'Will you youngsters forgive me if I leave you to finish off the night! I think everyone enjoyed themselves,' she added.

Stewart assured her that it had been a superlative success. 'I must tear myself away, and I'm sure Gavin will be leaving, also,' he added pointedly. 'Goodnight, Kate.' He stooped and kissed Kate's cheek. 'And thank you.' His expression was full of appreciation.

Gavin, subdued, almost stern, thanked her in turn. She left them, a smile on her face and a tear in her heart...knowing that behind Sara's bright appearance there was something wrong.

The drawing-room, after Kate left it, was filled with a silent ominous, waiting, as though the walls were leaning forward to catch every word uttered. Stewart said, 'It's very late, Gavin. I—' There was something unnerving in Gavin's expression that silenced him and made Sara look apprehensively from face to face.

'I'm not leaving,' Gavin said firmly, 'until Sara has answered a question I want to put to her.'

'Question?' Sara moistened her lips, her

235

mouth suddenly dry as uncertainty crept upon her.

'A very simple one,' Gavin said as his eyes met hers with mesmeric intensity. 'Are you *in love* with Stewart? If you are, then I have nothing further to say. Nothing whatever.'

Stewart cried in angry protest, 'My God, Gavin! How dare you have the impertinence to ask such a thing?'

Gavin persisted coolly, 'Let Sara speak for herself.'

Sara was in a whirlpool, as emotion ebbed and flowed, making her heart race and then seem to stop beating as she exclaimed, 'Stewart is right: the question is an impertinence. My feelings have nothing to do with you. I am engaged to Stewart and am going to marry him. *That* is my answer.' She gained courage from the statement and took a deep breath, avoiding Gavin's gaze, aware of his dynamic presence and the power of his personality.

There was a certain sternness that rang in Gavin's words, 'That is not an answer; that is an evasion. I don't want evasion, Sara. I want the truth. Do I have to ask the question again?'

'You have no right whatsoever to ask it,' she insisted.

'I am claiming that right for all our sakes.'

The silence that fell was heavy and dramatic as both men waited for her answer, and now Stewart was tense, fearful. Suddenly she sat there very still, knowing that she must tell the truth. Courage returned as she said with a quiet inevitability, 'I'm sorry, Stewart, I'm afraid my answer has to be no. I love you, but I am not in love with you.' Then eyes blazing, emotion almost choking her, she turned on Gavin, 'And now I repeat that my feelings have nothing to do with you. They never have, and they never *will*.'

CHAPTER TEN

Sara's words struck like thunder. Stewart moved to her chair and stood vigilantly beside it, addressing Gavin with threatening anger.

'Now, I hope you're satisfied. Get out of here.'

He might not have spoken as Gavin, ignoring him, said tensely, holding Sara's gaze, 'Your feelings have everything to do with me, because I'm in love with you and I intend to fight for you.' His voice was strong, firm and determined; he looked formidable as he faced her, wholly in command of the situation.

'In love with me,' Sara gasped, colour rising to her cheeks. 'But—' She stopped and squared her shoulders, defiance flashing in her eyes as she added, 'You have nothing to fight for.'

'That's for me to decide,' he retorted.

'I think not,' Stewart rapped out. 'You heard what Sara said. I'll also add that nothing she has told you in reference to me has changed my desire to marry her.' He added contemptuously, 'Since your sole objective was to smash things between us, you've failed utterly.'

Sara's gaze was drawn to Gavin because he exuded confidence, and a power undeniable as he said slowly and deliberately, 'My objective is to get to the truth. I don't need reminding of what Sara had to say. It is the reason for her saying it that concerns me. My fight, I suspect, begins with the lies I'm quite sure you've told her. And

I'm not going behind your back to tell her the truth.'

Sara began to tremble. She looked up at Stewart and a chill sensation of doubt crept upon her as she saw the expression of fear on his face.

'What do you mean—the truth about what?' she cried.

'About Marion—the past,' Gavin said quietly.

There was a sudden tense silence, which Stewart broke by rapping out, 'You wouldn't be so—so—'

'What, Stewart?' The words were like pistol shots. Gavin's expression was grim. 'I've suspected recently that you've lied about it.' He paused for a second and looked at Sara as he said with passionate earnestness, 'Stewart told you that Marion and I were lovers. Am I right?'

Stewart exclaimed, 'Look here, this is—'

'Am I *right?*' Gavin repeated sharply.

Sara looked at him unflinchingly.

'Yes,' she replied. 'And it wasn't difficult to believe since your relationship with her during her stay here certainly lent truth to the story.' She held her breath in suspense.

Gavin's voice rang with conviction,

'Marion and I were *never* lovers.'

'You don't have to defend yourself to me,' Sara cried. 'Your life is your own affair and I am certainly not the custodian of anyone's morals.' She struggled against the emotion tearing at her as she added, 'And what possible motive could Stewart have had for telling me—?' She paused, looking from face to face.

'His motive was to conceal his own involvement,' Gavin said.

'I've never heard such feeble nonsense in my life,' Stewart scoffed.

But Sara asked sharply, 'Then what *was* your motive?'

'I told you the truth because I wanted to warn and protect you,' Stewart said steadily. 'I told you, too, that Gavin had a power over women and would break your heart. He now admits he was in love with you. I think the least said the better.'

'That would be very convenient,' Gavin lashed out. He drew Sara's gaze to his. 'I was never Marion's lover,' he repeated, and the silence seemed to throb like the echo of muted drums, before he added, 'Stewart was the man in her life; the man who nearly wrecked her marriage and, this

240

time, I am not allowing him to escape the consequences.'

Sara's skin felt that it was lifting from her flesh as she cried in disbelief, '*Stewart!* Oh no,' she whispered. 'No.'

'I find no satisfaction in this scene,' Gavin said sombrely, 'but it was the only way in which I could tell the truth.'

Stewart began to protest, to bluster and then, defeated, flopped silent and wretched in the nearest chair.

'What Gavin says is true,' he said. 'But for him, I should have been struck off since Marion was my patient at the time of the affair. Her husband, Nigel, was suspicious and out for revenge. Gavin steered that suspicion away from me to himself. In the end he was instrumental in Marion and Nigel being reconciled. My being struck off would have killed my father and ruined my career.' He paused, then added regretfully, 'Basically I'm a weakling and I always hated Gavin's strength of character. At first, I desired you, and then fell in love with you, but I was afraid you would prefer Gavin, and wanted to convince you that he had been, and still was, involved with Marion. I knew he would never betray my past relationship with her, so I built up the story around him as an insurance policy if you like. At this moment I despise myself, but I'd probably do it again in similar circumstances.' He sighed, hesitated, and then added, 'There's just one other thing—'

Sara sat tense, shaking, hating herself because her love had not been great enough to allow her to give Gavin the benefit of the doubt.

'Becky was my daughter,' Stewart said tensely, '*That* was why Gavin was so protective towards her, and towards Marion. After all, Becky was his niece and he fought very hard in order that Nigel should accept her. Fortunately Nigel loved Marion sufficiently to forgive her.' He looked at Sara with a direct penetrating gaze. 'I'm telling you this because I always felt you suspected that Gavin was her father, in view of the lies I'd told you.'

Gavin looked appalled as he turned to Sara and asked, 'Is that true?'

She lowered her gaze for a second and then raised it as she answered honestly, 'Yes; yes, it is true. The possibility occurred to me on many occasions. It fitted naturally into the sequence of events, also your love for her—' The sentence died away significantly.

Stewart sighed; a deep regretful sigh. 'I've escaped payment all these years,' he said, 'but not any more. I congratulated myself on having manoeuvred everything very satisfactorily.' He squared his shoulders and got up from his chair. 'I've loved you, Sara,' he said humbly, 'more than I shall ever love any woman again; my punishment is that I've lost you. A punishment I deserve.' He looked straight into Gavin's eyes as he added, 'I wouldn't expect you ever to forgive what I tried to do to you, particularly after you saved me from disgrace in the first place.'

'I saved you for my father's sake,' Gavin said firmly, 'and was able to keep the whole sordid business from him. All I hope is that you'll conduct yourself with a little more integrity in future.'

Stewart didn't speak; he looked pale and ashamed as he said in a voice shaking with emotion, 'I shan't trouble either of you again.'

With that he walked from the room.

'I love you and I'm going to fight for you'.

Only the echo of those words rang in

Sara's ears during the silence that followed when she and Gavin were left alone; words that hardly seemed real, even as the scene she had just witnessed didn't seem real.

All she could think of to say tumbled out apologetically, appealingly, 'Forgive me for having misjudged you; but the evidence was so convincing...and—' she rushed on, 'it wasn't that I couldn't have understood your alleged relationship with Marion, but rather that it seemed I wasn't to be given the chance to understand.' Her voice broke, 'It was just the—the *circumstances.*' She lowered her gaze as she spoke.

'You could only have reacted as you did,' he commented generously. 'I see that now.'

But still at the back of her mind there lingered the memory of Marion's words the previous Christmas. It wasn't suspicion, now, but fear. Gavin hadn't been Marion's lover, but had he loved her?

'Why did Marion go away?' Sara asked.

Gavin gave a simple honest answer, 'Because, unfortunately, she was in love with me and I was not, and never had been, in love with her. Something I'd never suspected,' he admitted. 'I don't like discussing it, but I want you to know all the facts. When Marion came here, she did so in the hope that at some future date we could marry. My part in saving her marriage and Becky's future inspired in her some deep-rooted affection, gratitude, call it what you will, and she escaped into a fantasy world where she convinced herself that I shared her feelings, and that the past was a bond. I didn't realise this at first; it was only after Becky's death that the picture began to come into focus. The buying of Wyvern, my being involved in it; her dependence emotionally. It was like a wall being built around me, brick by brick. Then, when she began to need medical attention, I had to face the fact that only the truth—harsh though it was—could solve the problem. My lack of response was making her ill. She had talked of wanting to go to America to see her cousin, and almost took it for granted that I would leave the practice in your care and go with her.' He paused and sighed as he added, 'A woman finds it simple to tell a man she doesn't love him; a man almost feels a cad for doing so. And while I dislike going into these details, I want the slate wiped clean. My attitude, behaviour pattern during these past months reflected that inner turmoil; the intense dislike of hurting another human being, especially someone of whom I was genuinely fond; and to whom I was close because of Becky. I also felt protective because of all she had suffered through Stewart, no matter how foolish she might have been.' He looked at Sara very levelly as he went on, 'In some strange way I felt tied, almost as though she had become my responsibility. By the time I had resolved the situation and made her understand that I could never marry her, you were engaged to Stewart. Why,' he demanded, changing both his tone and attitude, 'did you agree to marry him, when you were not in love with him? *Why?*'

'Because I was so unhappy,' she replied without hesitation.

He looked shocked. 'Not as unhappy as I,' he countered harshly.

'*You!*' There was near disbelief in her voice.

'Loving you,' he retorted fiercely.

'A strange way you had of showing it! You never said one word, or even hinted!'

'Didn't I, Sara?' He held her gaze

masterfully. 'Didn't my arms tell you?'

'No,' she protested. 'They expressed your love of freedom, not of love itself.'

'Yours, too,' he reminded her. 'And there was Stewart in the background.'

'Just as there was Marion,' she said quietly.

He nodded. 'I hope I've made you understand that I had to resolve that problem before I felt free. I realise now how blind I was...and now?' He paused. '*Now*, Sara?' His voice dropped to a passionate whisper, 'Do you love me?' He moved to her side, his arms imprisoning her like a vice, 'Do you?'

She looked up at him, her eyes starry, 'Oh, yes,' she said on the breath of ecstasy, 'I love you; it seems that I always have.'

'Will you marry me?'

'Yes.' Her arms encircled his neck.

His kiss was deep and lingering, as though he would reach her heart.

She drew back, wonderingly, as she exclaimed, 'I would never have believed you would fight for any woman.' There was exultation in her voice.

'Believe me, I meant it,' he emphasised almost grimly, 'and you are not *any* woman. When I kissed you this evening

247

I was not merely obeying a desire to do so; I wanted to test your reactions.'

'I tried to resist you!'

'And succeeded in strengthening my resolution to fight!'

She looked up at him, seeing in that moment the man as he was when she first met him, and feeling the overwhelming attraction striking anew.

'I'd never make an actress,' she murmured, her voice low and full of happiness.

'You've put up a very good performance lately,' he reminded her with a smile, his gaze never once leaving her face. 'When will you marry me?'

'Tomorrow,' she said as desire flowed between them, adding swiftly, and with a little laugh, 'But we can't both get away at once!'

The absurdity amused him and he exclaimed, 'Norman will stand by, and I'll get a locum!'

They tensed at the prospect of being together—free from conflict.

'There's just one question I want to ask you,' she said.

'Only one, darling?'

'Yes; who was the woman you had in mind to replace me?'

For a second he had to think before answering, and then he gave a little indulgent laugh.

'Why—*you*,' he replied.

'Me?' There was amazed disbelief in her voice.

'I was conceited enough to believe, even then, that you would marry me,' he exclaimed. 'And quite determined to fight for you.'

'Oh, *Gavin*,' she said, colour rising to her cheeks, 'I haven't liked that woman a bit. I wondered if it was, well, someone—'

He put in as she stumbled over the sentence, 'Some former love? Some secret colleague?'

'I suppose so,' she admitted. 'I was all confused.'

'And now?'

'So delighted. Is the offer still open? We haven't discussed the practice side of things.'

'Do you still want to work with me?' His voice was serious.

'Yes; oh, yes...until we have children...'

'A honeymoon,' he suggested, after a pause.

'Somewhere in England,' she said simply. 'We've all our lives to see other countries, and I feel that I know so little of my own. No fuss; no flights; just the car in which we can disappear.' She looked up at him. 'Would you mind?'

'I'd love it and I know where I shall take you.'

'Where?'

'To a lovely hotel near Sherborne.'

'Dorset?' Her voice was eager.

'Yes; from there we can roam into Devon, Somerset, Cornwall—at our own pace, and on B roads so that we see England.' Gavin drew her back into his arms. 'Then you will be my *wife*,' he said tenderly, and with pride.

The word echoed between them with all the promise of tomorrow as his lips met hers.

The publishers hope that this book has given you enjoyable reading. Large Print Books are especially designed to be as easy to see and hold as possible. If you wish a complete list of our books, please ask at your local library or write directly to: Magna Large Print Books, Long Preston, North Yorkshire, BD23 4ND, England.

This Large Print Book for the Partially sighted, who cannot read normal print, is published under the auspices of

THE ULVERSCROFT FOUNDATION

THE ULVERSCROFT FOUNDATION

. . . we hope that you have enjoyed this Large Print Book. Please think for a moment about those people who have worse eyesight problems than you . . . and are unable to even read or enjoy Large Print, without great difficulty.

You can help them by sending a donation, large or small to:

**The Ulverscroft Foundation,
1, The Green, Bradgate Road,
Anstey, Leicestershire, LE7 7FU,
England.**
or request a copy of our brochure for more details.

The Foundation will use all your help to assist those people who are handicapped by various sight problems and need special attention.

Thank you very much for your help.

Other MAGNA Romance Titles
In Large Print

ROSE BOUCHERON
The Massinghams

VIRGINIA COFFMAN
The Royles

RUTH HAMILTON
Nest Of Sorrows

SHEILA JANSEN
Mary Maddison

NANCY LIVINGSTON
Never Were Such Times

GENEVIEVE LYONS
The Palucci Vendetta

MARY MINTON
Every Street